I0570860

RICH
&PETTY

RICH
&PETTY

By

Keesh

Felony Books, a division of Olive Group, LLC,
P.O. Box 484066, Kansas City, MO 64148

Copyright © 2025 by Keesh Washington

This book is a work of fiction. Names, characters, places, and incidents are products of the author's imagination or are used fictitiously. Any resemblance to actual events or locales or persons living or dead is entirely coincidental.

All rights reserved. No part of this book may be reproduced in any form or by any means without the prior written consent of the Publisher, excepting brief quotes used in reviews.

ISBN-13: 978-1-940560-37-3

Felony Books 2nd edition August 2025

10 9 8 7 6 5 4 3 2

Manufactured in the United States of America

For information regarding special discounts for bulk purchases, please contact Felony Books at info@felonybooks.com.

Books by Felony Books

AS A QUEEN THINKETH
AS A QUEEN THINKETH 2
AS A QUEEN THINKETH 3
MARRIED TO A DEMON
MARRIED TO A DEMON 2
MARRIED TO A DEMON 3
STATUS
STATUS 2
STATUS 3
SELFIE
RICH & PETTY
RICH & PETTY 2
RICH & PETTY 3
RICH & PETTY 4
TWO GIRLS ONE THUG VOL. 1
TWO GIRLS ONE THUG VOL. 2
TWO GIRLS ONE THUG VOL. 3
TRE POUND
TRE POUND 2
TRE POUND 3

and more ...

www.felonybooks.com

This book has **Corner Motion™**. Flip through the pages
fast and reveal a secret animation.

Corner Motion™ is a trademark of Olive Group, LLC.

Chapter 1: Phaedra Hodges

I was surprised that I didn't flinch when she ran her hand over my shoulder and down my bare back, as I crawled into bed with her. But her touch did give me an uneasy feeling.

This is the woman that has been sleeping with your husband for at least the past year, I reminded myself. *Phaedra, you don't have to do this.*

But the reality was—if I wanted to save my marriage, I *did* have to do this.

"Now kiss her," my husband ordered. He was on the bed naked too, upright on his knees, watching us with a greedy smile.

His mistress ran her hand down my shoulder to my elbow, where she gripped me and pulled me toward her gently. "Girl, don't act like I'm ugly," she said to me. "You gon' make me feel bad. C'mere, kiss me."

She wasn't bad looking. She had long hair, soft cocoa brown skin with the juiciest lips—and her body was flawlessly thick. You'd think she was surgically enhanced, but I was inches away from her flesh and I couldn't see one telling scar.

She started kissing me, then stopped.

"Relax," she said soothingly. "Imagine Isaiah isn't here right now. Just think of me and you."

Isaiah Hodges, my brawny handsome chocolate husband, spoke with less patience than her. "Kiss her, goddammit! Phaedra, quit acting like a fucking kid. You're 33 years old. You know how to fucking kiss. All of them little freaky ass porn stories you've been writing behind my back ... it's time to bring that shit to life, gotdammit."

"Those were just stories," I said, in a plea. "Isaiah, I've never done any of that before. I told you that. I just used my imagin—"

He raised his hand and I flinched, but he didn't hit me—this time. He just pointed at me, then at his beautiful mistress, exotic dancer Delana Cobbins.

"Kiss her, before you piss me off," he growled.

"Phaedra, you might as well get it over with," Delana said in a nasal tone. "We all know what happens if you don't. It won't be so bad, trust me. My mouth is clean."

Clean? I highly doubt it, I said to myself. *Dirty bitch. Dirty, home-wrecking—*

Isaiah suddenly grabbed the back of my head, fisting my hair in a bunch, as he snapped his fingers at his stripper with his free hand and demanded she kiss me now. She did, and then he joined in on the kiss too.

This is how it began. An uncoordinated three-way kiss.

It was sloppy, and I was trying to kiss more of Isaiah than Delana but she kept trying to stick her tongue in my mouth. Thankfully, Isaiah pushed me down on the bed, flat on my back, as he climbed on top of me.

"You ready for this big dick, Phae," he said to me breathlessly.

"Uh-huh," I said, nodding.

I was staring at his massive dick as he pushed it inside of me. I was only somewhat wet so he had to pull out a few times, spit on his dick and push back in deeper.

"Look at that big ol' black thang," Delana said, out of turn. "Get it in that pussy, Isaiah. Get it in there. Fuck her ass hard, boy."

Once his momentous thrusts got underway, I finally started to relax. I was no longer thinking about marriage and infidelity and friends and family finding out about tonight— I just wanted Isaiah to make me cum.

"Oooh!" I moaned, as he spanked into my wet pussy.

Then I felt a set of lips on my right nipple, then a hand squeezing my whole breast in a way that electrified my entire body. It was Delana; she had squeezed underneath Isaiah to tongue my chest down.

I was surprised that it turned me on even more.

"I love your titties, girl," she said to me, sucking and licking around my aureoles with the tip of her tongue. "They're so big and succulent. I'd pay for titties this big."

She bit my nipple and I hissed. She laughed.

Isaiah was still giving me the business. His big dick was sliding in and out of me now with no effort. He was hammering me, brutalizing me, his ballsack smacking against my vagina.

I heard Delana say something to Isaiah but I was so out of it that I didn't catch it. Apparently she wanted more action, because Isaiah scooted back and let her position herself in front of me. She lowered her sexy face between my legs, and as soon as her top lip even grazed across my pussy lips—coupled with the stream of heat from her breath—it gave me wonderful butterflies.

"Uh-uhhhh-uh-uhhhh," I shuddered.

"This is my pussy now," she said.

She was teasing me—licking my inner womanness, then blowing it softly to immediately cool me off. But as soon as my husband entered her from behind, the teasing stopped. He fucked her so hard he pushed her forehead against my pussy folds.

It hurt. I winced.

Delana looked back at him. "Easy, nigga," she snarled at him. "You see me trying to do my thing. Back the fuck up."

I actually felt some kind of suppressed female empowerment glow inside of me after she talked to him like that. I had never called my husband the n-word, let alone during sex.

And when he actually listened to her and slowed his pumps—no backtalk, no physical abuse, no threats—I thought, *Is that all it takes to put a man in check?*

Delana ate my pussy like it had never been eaten before. It felt like she had full control of every nerve in my body, and I couldn't understand how—because all she was using was her tongue and her lips, and a minutiae of respiration. I was fucking *paralyzed*. It was as if she was kinetically sending signals of joy through her tongue, that my brain was beginning to interpret as love.

Does Delana love me?

"Time to switch this shit up," Isaiah's deep voice interrupted. "Yall change positions. Hurry the fuck up before my dick go soft. Delana, on yo back. Phaedra, c'mere. Come toot that ass in the air."

As we were trading places, me and Delana bumped foreheads and we all got a good laugh out of it. For once since this threesome commenced, I actually started to feel like the three of us were a team. I wasn't looking at it like I was the wife under duress, forced to have sex with her husband and his side chick. This was feeling like three adults having a good time. Grown folks getting it on.

"*Ssss,*" I hissed when Isaiah entered me from behind. After five years of marriage I still hadn't gotten accustomed to his size.

In front of me, halfway under me, was Delana. She was so utterly beautiful, so much better-looking than any protagonist I had ever created in my head. My titties waggled over her pussy as Isaiah fucked me senseless.

Delana looked at me expectantly, then said, "What are you waiting for? Show me what you got, Mrs. Hodges."

It registered late—*She wants me to eat her pussy. Oh my God!* I looked down at it. Her folds were gnarled, messy-looking, uninviting, several different shades of pink with areas growing black. Her labia was poking out further than I thought it should have.

But, being fair, her pussy smelled like roses.

"You're going too hard, Isaiah," she said to my husband. "How the fuck do you expect a bitch to get her pussy ate and you behind her going ham? Let her taste my goods first, you selfish muthafucka."

"Fuck you, bitch," he said as pumped in and out of me. But he did ease off a little.

"No, *fuck you,*" she spit. "You had her all to yo'self long enough." She eyed me seductively. "I always wanted to get eaten out by a writer."

It felt good hearing her call me a writer. I hadn't published anything yet, but I had several short stories on my computer, complete and ready to submit ... if I ever gained the courage to. My lack of courage stemmed from my stories' content, not sure how editors would receive me. I wrote a lot about sex. Boy on girl, girl on girl, and I had just recently started to explore group sex. Isaiah actually found and read a couple of my racy stories and he beat my ass because he thought they were a part of my daily diary. He thought I was cheating on him and documenting it.

Now, as I stared at this unique pussy below me, I felt like a novice. In practice, I was. But in my mind, I had eaten pussy so many times—

Thwack! Isaiah smacked my ass cheek hard as hell. I gritted my teeth in pain as he continued to fuck me.

"Eat that pussy, bitch," he said angrily, thrusting harder. "Hurry up. I got a lot planned for you hoes tonight."

Delana rolled her eyes. "She's thinking too hard. She's not gonna do it, Isaiah. Fuck it, I'll wait." She laid all the way back against the sheets, tucking her arms behind her head.

Thwack!

"Eat that pussy," he commanded. "Don't act like you don't know how. All them goddamn freaky-ass stories you been hiding ..."

"I'm not ready," I said with my eyes closed. "I can't."

He grunted out, "Yes you can."

"You eat her out," I said. "I'll watch."

He must have mistaken what I said as a smart remark, because in a flash he snatched me sideways by my hair and yanked me off the bed. I fell on the floor, hurting my elbow and my shoulder.

He towered over me quick, with balled fists. "What the fuck did you say to me, bitch? You call yo'self tellin' me what the fuck to do?"

"No!" I said vehemently. "I'm sorry, I didn't mean it like that, Isaiah. I was just suggesting—"

He cut me off, turning to Delana. "Get my belt," he told her.

"No!" I screamed.

Delana hopped out of the king-sized bed giddily, and I realized the bond I thought we were building was just a figment of my imagination.

She slipped the belt out of his frumpled slacks and came over and handed it to him. "You gon' beat her ass fareal?" she asked him, smiling.

Isaiah ignored her. Then to me: "Get'cho ass up and get back on that bed."

"Don't hit me," I pleaded.

"Get up."

"You ain't gon' hit her, nigga," Delana said. She was instigating. "You don't be beatin' this bitch like you say you do. You ain't 'bout that life."

"Get up," he said to me again.

"Just don't hit me," I pleaded. "I'll do it. I'll eat her pussy."

I slowly got to my feet. I was showing him my palms, giving my surrender when—*Shwack!*—he whipped me just below the buttocks, and the pain lanced through me like a lightning strike. It was so overbearing it dropped me back to my knees.

Shwack!—another whip. Across the middle of my back. Delana squealed louder than I did. But my squeal was one of intense pain; hers was pure delight.

"Oh shit!" she said. "She just be taking that shit, huh?"

Isaiah was huffing. "Get. Up."

I started crying. And when I saw Delana hug him from the back, reaching around to stroke his semi-erect penis, I knew this was all a part of their plan. Isaiah was showing off his dominance over me to impress his stripper. This turned her on.

I was trembling as I made my way to my feet again. I knew it was coming before he cocked his hand back.

Shwack! Shwack! Shwack!

He beat me bloody, just like I knew he would. But I nearly died inside when he handed the belt to Delana. "Your turn," he said to her. "Wrap one end of the belt around your knuckles."

She did as she was told, leaving about three feet of the belt's slack hanging down to the floor. "Like this?" she asked him.

"Just like that. Now let that bitch have it."

Delana looked down at me and grinned. Dangling the belt slack over her shoulder, she flinched at me. When I cowered in fear, she burst out laughing. I started to smile too, thinking, *She's not gonna really hit me.* But that was when she swung the belt with all her might.

Shwack!

Chapter 2: Phaedra Hodges

Two Years Later

"I know you probably hear this a lot, but I really am your number one fan," the young girl said to me, as I sat at the table signing my name in what felt like the thousandth book.

I started scribbling a little message under my signature that would read: *To my number one fan.* But I barely got through the word "number" when the girl added:

"I knew you didn't kill your husband and his mistress," she said to me. I looked up and met her eyes. "That's what the book was about, right? You telling everybody that it wasn't you, that it was one of his other side chicks that killed them."

"Ma'am, please," I said. "It was listed out front before you came in. No personal questions."

"I'm sorry. I just think it was brilliant how you wrote it."

I lowered my head and finished the note, then I closed the hardback book and handed it to her. "Thank you for coming out and showing your support," I said.

"Picture?" she asked.

I forced a smile. "Sure."

I was tired. I could barely keep my eyes open, and there was still at least another forty people standing in line waiting for my autograph. I remembered dreaming of this day—published author, New York Times bestseller, fans in line stretching out the door—and now that it was here I was dreading it.

My very first book signing, on the other hand, was exhilarating. It was held here at this location as well, the Atlanta-Fulton Public Library off Williams Street. I didn't live too far from here.

The next reader in line handed me his sticky note with his handwritten name on it. But before I even looked at the name, I found myself staring up at him with a curious eye. He was handsome, tall, brown-skinned, wearing a debonair navy blue suit with the pocket handkerchief peeking out. His cuff links sparkled.

With a nervous smile, he dusted off the lapels of his blazer. "Somethin' on me? Why are you staring at me like that?"

"Sorry ..." I said, looking down at the sticky note. "... Rayshawn? Did I pronounce that right?"

"Yes, ma'am."

"My apologies again for staring. I'm just not used to grown men showing up to my book signings. As you can see behind you, roughly ninety percent of my readers are women."

He glanced behind him for my benefit, then he reached in the inside pocket of his blazer and pulled out a business card and held it out to me.

I didn't accept it. "What is that?" I asked him with attitude.

"It's a business card with my contact info on it. I'm a producer for one of the biggest independent film companies in Atlanta. I'd like to talk to you later about turning your novel into a feature film."

I crossed my arms on the table and gave him a smug grin. "You must not have read the sign outside either. No personal questions and no soliciting."

"This isn't soliciting. This is a ticket to vast opportunity." He shook the card. "Just take it. Please, Ms. Hodges."

I shook my head no.

He considered his options for a moment, then he dropped the card on the table. "Well sign my book then. Can you do that much?"

"Did you even read the book?" I asked him, as I wrote *To Rayshawn* in his hardback copy of my book titled *Petty*. I autographed it in one fancy stroke. I handed him the novel. "Did you?"

"No personal questions please," he replied smartly, then walked off.

I let out a dry laugh. *Men are so petty,* I thought.

After I signed the last book from the last fan standing in line, I leaned back in my chair and exhaled a great big exhaustive sigh of relief. "It's *overrrr,"* I sang.

My publicist, an older white lady with shoulder-length blond hair, interrupted my moment of peace. "Phaedra, we need to talk about the next event," she said.

"No, we don't."

"Yes, we do," she threw back sharply.

Her name was Sarah Maturo. She was a bony woman, so frail that, when I first met her, I thought she was suffering from some kind of terminal illness. Her skin was rubbery and pocked with light traces of liver spots.

But she dressed nice and smelled good. Today her suit was basic but she wore this gold necklace with a pearl pendant that sat beautifully against her sunken chest. And her six-inch dress sandals were classy and ageless.

"If you want to garner new readers and increase your fanbase, you have to travel more often," she said. "You can't expect all of your fans to hop on a plane to Atlanta every time."

"Where do you want me to go now?"

"North Carolina."

"Why there?"

"Because we've been tracking your sales and there's been a large spike in Charlotte. But I want you to hit Charlotte, Raleigh, and Greensboro. Three days, Phaedra. Just three days. That's all the publisher is asking from you."

"That's all the publisher is asking from me this month," I corrected her. "But what about next month?"

"Next month ... Canada, then Chicago."

I sighed again. All I wanted to do was sit inside my big Atlanta home and lose myself within the pages of a good book not written by me. A glass of wine maybe, while a random Atlien thug boy sucked my toes. This was wishful thinking though, because the demands of bestsellerdom were calling my name.

My blood sister was standing to the right of me, retracting the banner stand that displayed my book. "It's okay," Patricia West said to me. "Hit the road. Get that money. I'll take care of home."

"Are you sure?" I asked her.

"Yeah. I can handle it."

My sister lived with me inside the half a million dollar home that I had once shared with my husband. After he disappeared, she moved in with me to help maintain the place. Yard work, trash days, cooking, cleaning—she either did these things herself or coordinated with outside help to get it done. She was my shoulder to lean on.

Patricia was a big ol' girl—a *real* BBW, not the thick kind—and she wore her hair in flowing crinkles. She also liked long, colorful stiletto fingernails, as opposed to my nude acrylics.

And she had never been married. This was a status I wished I had held onto.

"Thank you, Patricia," my publicist said to her. "You're a Godsend."

"No problem, Sarah. I know I can't keep Phaedra all to myself. Unfortunately I have to share her with the world."

"Oh shut up," I said to my sister playfully. "You're gonna be glad to see me go."

She laughed.

I stood up and yawned. I was tired, but not too tired to miss the party at Club Crucial tonight. I needed some new penis. I promised myself I wasn't going to sleep tonight without it.

Chapter 3: Phaedra Hodges

"What about him?" Patricia suggested to me, as she slyly pointed to a table of black men sitting not too far from us. "He has an ungodly big package. I can tell. Look."

I laughed at her. "How can you tell? You can't even see his feet."

"I don't need to. That's where bitches go wrong, judging a nigga's dick game by the size of his feet. Nope. It's all in the shoulders." She tapped her right shoulder, then her left with the same hand. "It's all about the width. And that man over there has shoulders wider than Frankenstein's."

I cracked up laughing. "You need to write a book on the silly telltale signs you be coming up wit'."

"You know, I thought about it." She put a finger on her chin, pretending to contemplate. Then with the same finger, she pointed at me. "But you're the writer. You gon' put it together for me?"

"No," I said, crinkling my nose. "I don't write nonfiction. I write fiction. But then again, your book would be considered fiction because you don't have a clue when it comes to sex. You ain't had dick in how long?"

She flipped me off and we shared another good laugh.

Club Crucial was jam-packed. There were so many beautiful young people in here dancing, smoking weed, and having a good time under the many spotlights. There was a boxing ring in the middle of the club, where a DJ was announcing a new up-and-coming Atlanta rapper. Girls laughed and took selfies. Well-dressed thugs walked around with gold chains and stacks of rubber banded money—*openly*, not at all scared of getting robbed. They dapped each other and posed for impromptu pictures with the girls. About thirty minutes ago someone threw a wad of one-dollar bills in the air for no apparent reason. There were a few bills still stuck in the bar joists overhead.

Love was brewing here. And I wanted to leave with my portion.

A waitress came to our table with a gold bottle of champagne. "This is for you, Phaedra."

Most of the waitresses here knew my first name. Not all of them knew I was a writer, but they knew I wasn't a run-of-the-mill clubgoer. I was a regular, but I was a high-paying regular.

"I don't remember ordering another drink." I looked at Patricia in confusion. "Did you order this?"

She shook her head no. We already had two bottles at our table and one hadn't even been opened yet.

The waitress said, "This is a complimentary bottle. It came from a man named ..." She thought for a moment. "I forgot his name. Tall guy. Cute. He's wearing a well-made suit."

I looked past the waitress, trying to see if I could spot him. Not too many people were wearing suits in here.

"You can't see him from here," she explained. "He's on the other side of the club, sitting at the bar. He said you knew him."

I looked at the bottle of Ace of Spades. It was one of the pricier drinks here. Whoever sent it may not have been rich but they surely weren't broke.

My husband was well-off and he cheated on me and beat my ass every chance he got. Not to say that whoever sent the bottle would try to do me like that—*hell no, I wasn't putting up with that treatment ever again!*—but tonight I had a taste for a struggling savage. I wanted to take a boy home who still lived with his mother, someone who couldn't spell *goal,* a nigga who lived to fuck and fucked to live. I could bust my nut, give him a hundred dollars and usher his ass back out of my life.

"Send it back please," I said to the waitress. "Tell him thanks but no thanks. I got enough to sip on as it is."

"No problem," she said, confiscating the bottle. "You two fine ladies enjoy your night."

After the waitress left, Patricia asked me if I wanted her to go fetch the brotha "with the Frankenstein shoulders." I told her yes and she took a quick sip of some champagne from a wine glass and then wobbled off. I loved how she loved to love me and take care of me. She was a true sister. To think, when we were kids we used to fight over the stupidest stuff.

Moments later Patricia returned to the table, arm in arm with a young man who looked to be in his early twenties. He was wearing a small gold chain, and the collar of his black tee shirt was crinkled, as if he'd been chewing on it. He smelled like weed.

Just the type of thug I was looking for, I thought, smiling inside. I sipped some champagne.

"This is Lil Zoney," Patricia said to me, holding in a laugh. "He's an aspiring rapper. Zoney, this is my little sister Phaedra Hodges. She writes make-believe books with steamy sex scenes. And she wants to fuck you tonight."

The boy stared at her, openmouthed. He chuckled, then he looked at me as if this was a joke.

"She's telling the truth," I said to him with a straight face. "I come here often, for one purpose and one purpose only—to find a young man with some stamina that knows how to use it. Are you that man?"

He looked between the both of us again, still not believing his luck. I had this problem a lot, unfortunately. I scared a lot of young men off with my brazenness. But I didn't know any other way.

"What are yall tryna pull?" he asked us. Then he singled me out: "No disrespect, shawty, but you're too beautiful to be a ho."

"Awwww," I gushed, intertwining my hands near my chin and tilting my head like a schoolgirl. "That's one of the sweetest things I've ever heard." Then I got serious. "Sit down, Zoney," I ordered.

He was hesitant, so Patricia shoved him forward. He finally sat down and I scooted close to him. Patricia sat on the other side of him, boxing him in.

"Did you drive here?" I asked him.

"No, I rode with a couple of my boys."

"Can you get a ride over to Tuxedo Park tonight?"

His eyes got wide. "Them is some big ol' houses over there. You live over there?"

"Yes. Can you find a ride?"

"I got a Chevy that runs good. It's clean on the inside. But I didn't drive it tonight because my tags ain't right."

"In my neighborhood, it's risky driving without legit registration, but if you can make it ..." I took his hand and guided it between my legs, underneath my skirt, letting his fingertips graze the meaty lips of my pussy through the fabric of my thong. "... You'll get to play with this kitty kat all night long. If you treat her right, I'll put you on my list of callbacks."

"Shit, I'll walk there if I have to," he said excitedly.

I wrote down my address on a napkin and told him to be at my house at 1 a.m. sharp. Then he asked for a sip of Ace of Spades because he'd never tried it before and I told him he could take the unopened bottle with him.

"Wait," Patricia said, stopping him from getting up.

"What?" he asked.

"You have one more test to pass."

I rolled my eyes. I knew Patricia was just trying to help, but I hadn't had penis inside me in a week and I was craving it. Pass or fail, Lil Zoney was coming home with me tonight.

"I'm game," Zoney said, smiling. "What's the test?"

"It's the girth test," said Patricia. "I wrap my hand around your dick and stroke it until you're nice and hard, and if my thumb can touch my fingers, you lose. If not, you get to have sex with a bestselling author."

He laughed. "Why can't your sister perform the test, if she's the one I'ma be fucking?" he asked Patricia. I sipped some more champagne.

"Because her fingers are longer than mine," she answered. "Most men lose if she does it."

He stared at her, then me—I gave him a good luck smile—and then he proceeded to unfasten his jeans. Under the table, Patricia helped him pull his dick out and then she set out to do her deed—she started jacking him off. To my surprise, Lil Zoney wasn't so little after all; his brown phallus began to lengthen and expand well beyond her grip. Her fingers couldn't touch; instead they formed the letter C.

"Let me try," I said, eagerly taking ahold of his meat. My fingers were borderline but not quite touching. If I squeezed him hard enough, they might've touched. But I didn't want to hurt the boy. *Not yet anyway.* "This thang is beautiful, Zoney."

"Thank you," he said.

Needless to say, he passed. But I didn't want to let his shaft go. And neither did Patricia. It reminded me of when we were kids, sharing a new toy.

"Don't bend it so much," I warned Patricia.

"I'm not. Zoney, am I hurting you?" she asked.

"Nah. Yall good."

I firmed my grip, getting my fingertips to finally touch. "Did that hurt?" I asked him.

He shook his head no, smiling.

"What's going on over here?" asked a new voice.

All three of us looked up. I was surprised to see the man in the nice suit that had showed up to my book signing earlier. Rayshawn. He was standing in front of our table, hands stuffed in his slacks pockets as if we owed him something.

"Are you following me?" I asked him.

"Yes," he said.

I blinked. I didn't expect him to say that. Me and Patricia were both still holding onto Lil Zoney's erection.

"I'm following you on social media," Rayshawn told me. "You shared with the world a couple hours ago that you'd be here tonight."

I looked over at Patricia. She had control over my social media page.

Patricia nodded. "I did make a post," she confirmed.

Staring back at Rayshawn, I said, "What do you want? A picture with me?"

"First, I just want to know why you declined to accept the bottle of champagne I sent over here."

"As you can see, we already have drinks available. Thanks but no thanks."

"First, you turn down my business card. Then you turn down my drink. I'm starting to think you don't like me."

"Maybe she doesn't," Patricia butted in. "Have you thought about that?"

Rayshawn looked at her. "I almost called you out your name. Speak when spoken to."

"Who the fuck are you?!" she hollered at him.

Lil Zoney spoke up for us. "Ay, shawty, I don't know what time you on," he said to Rayshawn in a deep, aggressive voice, "but I think you should be on yo merry way. These ladies belong to me."

Rayshawn looked at me and Patricia, then Zoney, then me again, and he chuckled. "Do you still have my card?" he asked me, as if he was somehow more important than Zoney.

"No," I said.

"I threw it away," Patricia said.

"Phaedra, may I give you another card please? I really think if we sit down and talk, you'll be very excited about working with me and my team on turning your novel into a motion picture. Just one conversation, that's all I'm asking."

I liked Rayshawn's persistence. I really did. It was hard for me to say no to a man that exuded so much confidence and effort to spend time with me, even though his intentions seemed strictly professional. Confidence and effort was what attracted me to my ex-husband.

But I already had my catch for the night.

"You're rubbing me the wrong way, sir," I said to him. "You insulted my sister and you're insulting Lil Zoney by interrupting his time with us. If you don't leave, I'm gonna call security. And they know me personally here. So that means when they drag you out of here and fuck you up, it'll be personal."

Rayshawn's lips formed a tight line. His tongue wormed across his lower teeth, causing his bottom lip to protrude. I could tell he didn't like being told no.

Just like Isaiah, I thought.

Finally, he said, "You all have a nice night. Sorry to bother you." He gave a curt wave and walked off.

I found myself watching him leave longer than I should have, for some reason. He had left an impression on me, and his strong presence stirred in my stomach long after he was gone.

Together, me and Patricia's drunk asses played with Lil Zoney's thickness until he shot cum at the underside of the table. Some of it oozed into my palm and over my knuckles and I showed Patricia how much of his semen I had on my hand and she showed me her palm—more cum than me—and we all cracked up laughing. We sent Lil Zoney on his way, but not before reminding him to be at my Tuxedo Park address no later than 1 a.m.

Me and Patricia didn't stay long after that. We got up and made our way outside. In the parking lot, as we approached my Porsche Panamera, we saw someone leaning over the hood of it. It didn't take long to notice it was the producer Rayshawn. He was sticking his business card under one of my windshield wipers.

"Hey!" Patricia shouted. "Get the fuck away from my sister's car!"

Rayshawn turned to us. From his smile, I knew he could care less that he'd been caught. Patricia started going in her purse for her knife—the blade was under five inches so it was legal in Georgia—but I stopped her by grabbing her arm.

"You just don't know how to take no for an answer, do you?" I said to him.

"No, ma'am. When I know what I want, there's no such thing as no."

"Give me your fucking card," I said, exasperated.

"You want it?"

"Yes."

He slipped it out from underneath my windshield wiper and handed it to me. I read it: *Rayshawn Meeks, The Best Film Producer in the South.*

"So what is it exactly that you want to talk to me about?" I asked him.

"I want to turn your novel into a movie. I want to see what your direction is. Have you even thought about turning it into a movie?"

"What author hasn't?"

"Well, I'm your man."

"I have a lot of questions to ask you."

"You have the number. Give me a call any time."

"What about right now?"

His eyebrows went up. "Right now? Here?"

"At my house," I said. "Tonight. Right now. You have a car, right? We can talk on the way there."

Patricia seemed worried. "No, not him, Phaedra."

I gave her a tight-lipped glare for her to shut the hell up. This was my life.

Rayshawn looked at Patricia. "Not me what?"

"Never mind her. Do you want to help make my dreams come true or not?"

He licked his lips. "Let's ride," he said.

Chapter 4: Rayshawn Meeks

"Nice car," she said.

"Thank you. I just bought it."

I was driving a 2017 Bentley GT. Actually, it was a rental, rented out under the name of the film company I was currently working with. The action scene that this Bentley was shot in was finished and it still had two days left under the contract, so I took it out for a spin. But Phaedra didn't need to know that. Details had a tendency to ruin dreams.

"Tuxedo Park," I stated, glancing over at her as I drove. "Books must be doing pretty good, huh?"

"Yes, among other things."

"Other things? Are you an investor? You into stocks n' shit?"

"How is that relevant to my novel?"

"Sorry, just tryna get to know you. Casual conversation, you know?"

I drove on, asking her questions about actors and actresses that she'd like to see in her adaptation. She threw out a few celebrity names, some of which I actually had contact information for—Wendy Raquel Robinson, Daniel Kaluuya, Bokeem Woodbine, Jada Pinkett Smith. The biggest hurdle with Phaedra seemed like it would be convincing her publishing company to let us purchase her story. They owned half the rights.

A moment later, we were pulling up to her circle drive. Her house—or more accurately, her mansion—had a classic appeal. It was a mixture of brick and white stonework, with a fir-studded front yard and a couple of white columns supporting the front porch.

"How big is your estate?" I asked her. "Or can I not ask that because it's not book-related?"

"It's five acres. The house is about eight thousand square foot."

"I bet you don't got a pool, though."

She chuckled. "Would you like to come in and find out?"

Hell yeah, you sexy muthafucka! was my first thought. But she couldn't be inviting me in to hit that pussy because her Porsche was parked in front of us. Her sister was here. She had beat us home.

I gave her a side eye. "Um ... sure? I guess."

"Nervous?" she asked.

"Uh, duh," I said, as if it should have been obvious. "You go from shutting my business card down over and over, making me feel like a complete stalker, to inviting me in your home after midnight. Wouldn't you be nervous?"

"Probably."

"It's kind of late," I said. "If you want to know more about the step-by-step process of going from book to screenplay to finished film, then we need to sit down with my business partner, Faheem Mathis. I can set something up for tomorrow, or first thing Monday—"

"I want to have sex with you," she said, cutting me off.

I was at a loss for words. I looked ahead at her Porsche again.

"Don't worry about my sister," she said. "It's a big house. She won't hear us."

"You're a beautiful woman, Phaedra, but I don't wanna mess up a possible business relationship."

"We won't. We can walk and chew gum. We're both grown, right?" she said.

"Right."

"Before you came along, I had planned to have sex with the boy you saw me and my sister with at the club. Lil Zoney. But then your persistence sort of turned me on. At first your whole persona reminded me of somebody that I didn't want to be reminded of, but now for some reason I'm turned on by you."

"You're serious, aren't you?"

"I love intimacy and its counterpart—*fucking*. You've read my novel, haven't you?"

I hesitated. "Yes," I lied.

"Then you should have an idea of the type of sex that I Iike. I didn't put six sex scenes inside of an eighty-thousand-word manuscript because I'm shy."

In no way did I plan to turn this woman down. I was just flustered, that's all. I had been aggressively approached by chicks in the past, but never by a woman as successful as Phaedra Hodges.

Or as sexy.

"If you wait too long, I'm locking the front door," she warned me, as she opened my passenger door and climbed out.

I was still looking for the catch. *But what if there isn't one?* I had learned that, in business, when you prepare yourself for an opportunity and then opportunity arrives, people call it luck. The same could be applied to sex. I looked good. I was dressed nice, my hair was cut, I was a little out of shape but I was still agile, and I had prepared myself for sex with a bestselling author by piping down all the skanks and scallywags in my past.

This wasn't luck. This was preparation crashing head-on into opportunity.

Quickly, I hopped out of the Bentley and jogged over to the mansion steps. "Hold up, Phae. I'm comin', don't lock it!"

Chapter 5: Rayshawn Meeks

"So your sister lives here with you," I asked, as I stared at the vastly spacious foyer and the spiral staircase leading to the second floor.

Behind me, I heard the front door lock quietly. *Clack.*

Then Phaedra was suddenly passing me and walking down a hallway. "Yes, Patricia lives with me. C'mon."

I followed her to the kitchen, where her sister was preparing a small snack. The big woman had a butter knife in her hand, and to her left was a jar of Miracle Whip.

I noticed that Phaedra was confused by the late-night meal, but then her expression cleared as if she and her sister shared some kind of secret understanding.

"He's hungry?" Phaedra asked her.

"Yep," her sister said curtly.

"This late? He's not sleep."

"Nope."

I said, "Yall got pets?"

Both of the girls looked at me.

"I don't do dogs," I added nervously. "I got bit by one when I was little."

"Don't worry," Phaedra said to me. "He's in the basement. We're gonna be upstairs."

"Phaedra, may I ask you a question please?" her sister said.

"What is it?"

"A private question. Can I talk to you alone in the living room?"

Phaedra sighed. Then she told me to give them a minute alone, as she and Patricia left the kitchen.

I looked at my Rolex watch. It was 12:42 a.m. I was supposed to be on set at the studio at 5 a.m., but according to how long I lasted inside of Phaedra, I wasn't so sure I was going to make it to work on time. I was planning to waddle in her pussy.

With my elbows on the island counter, I looked around at all of the stainless steel appliances. "Nice set up," I said to myself. "This woman got her shit together."

I went over to the refrigerator and opened the door. I was surprised to see that it was stuffed full. There was no neatness or organization to it whatsoever.

"They got enough food in here to make it through a nuclear holocaust. I bet I know which sister does the shopping," I said, with a dry laugh. "Damn, they do got all the goodies though. Fresh grapes, Dr. Pepper, leftover Chinese ..."

I grabbed a single-serve bottle of apple juice, cracked it open and took a sip. Then I put it back where I got it and closed the door.

I waited for a few minutes for the girls to come back. Then, impatiently, I walked into the hallway and then into the living room, where I thought they were talking.

But the living room was empty.

I did, however, see something strange peeking out from under the couch. It looked like some kind of wooden board. I squatted down and pulled it out; it was a tray. And it held a black velvet box. I opened it and saw a magnificent diamond ring inside. It looked like a wedding ring or an engagement ring. Inscribed in the jewel's milky stone was the letters I and D.

What does this stand for? I thought. *And why is it hiding underneath the furniture?*

I closed the box, scooting the tray back under the couch, and then I stood back up.

"What are you doing in here?" Phaedra asked me.

"I was looking for you and your sister," I said.

"Don't you know it's impolite to wander around someone's house unescorted?"

"Yeah. It's just as impolite as leaving a guest in the kitchen alone forever."

"Forever? Really, Rayshawn? I was gone like five minutes."

"Five minutes away from you is like forever."

I could tell she was trying not to smile. She turned away from me before she broke. "Follow me," she said.

We went up the spiral staircase and we passed a portrait of her and a man that I assumed was her husband. I got nervous.

"You're not married, are you?" I asked her.

Almost to the top of the stairs, she stopped and turned. At our angle, she was looking down at me. "No, I'm not married. What kind of woman do you think I am?"

A nympho, I thought. But I kept my answer to myself.

"I *was* married," she said. "But I'm not married anymore. I thought you read my book."

"Yeah, but I thought it was fiction."

"It is. But some parts are true."

I followed her into the master bedroom, where my eyes roamed over luxury and elegance. In the center of the room, against the wall, sat a big California king bed with a brown leather button-tufted headboard. In front of it was an antique Kashan area rug.

I whistled in fascination. "I bet you sleep good *every* night, huh?"

"You'd be surprised," she said.

Then, in the corner of the room close to the ceiling, I saw a tiny black dot recessed in the beige-colored sheetrock. I knew what it was immediately.

"Is that a camera?" I asked her.

"Huh?"

I pointed. "Right there in the corner. Up there."

She looked, and she acted as if she just now noticed it. "Oh yeah, I guess that is a camera."

"You guess?"

"My husband set up a hidden camera in this room. It's been there forever, I forgot about it. He thought I was cheating. Have you heard of cheater's paranoia?"

"No. Is it a movie?"

I shook my head no. "Uh-uhn. It's a psychology term for people who cheat. Most cheaters suffer from paranoia. They automatically go to great lengths to catch their spouses or significant others cheating, when in most cases they're the only ones involved in an affair. My husband suffered from cheater's paranoia."

"Is the camera on?" I asked.

"No. It's not hooked up anymore."

Then she kicked off her heels and climbed into bed, turning on her butt so she sat facing me. She leaned back on her elbows, leaving one knee bent.

"Take me, Johnathan," she said breathlessly, as she flipped her hair over her shoulder.

I laughed. "Who's Johnathan?"

"I don't know. That's my classic romance movie impersonation."

"You got any 'hood movie impressions?"

"Okay," she said, smiling. Then her voice deepened: *"Come get this pussy, nigga."*

I chuckled, as I began unbuttoning my blazer. "You ain't said nothing but a word, Felicia," I said, letting the jacket fall to the floor.

As soon as I got in bed with her, she started rolling her panties down her thighs. Any doubts I had that she wasn't really going to let me fuck tonight flew out the door. I helped her take her panties off, then flipped her skirt up and snatched her toward me by her thighs.

I started eating her pussy.

It didn't dawn on me that her cum had oozed in my mouth until I swallowed; it was a thick creamy flood that tickled my throat on its way down.

I kept licking, sucking her clit, trying to fill my mouth with her juices again.

She moaned, *"Ooohh,* nigga, you ain't playin'. *Ssss ... ooohhh ..."*

I curled two fingers inside of her, petting her inner love button while salivating over her clit. She screamed, threw her head back, clawed the sheets. Her juices poured out. What I couldn't swallow I let overflow down my chin, leaving sticky deposits on her sheets.

I kept tongue-kissing her succulent pearl, treating her pinkness with moments of delicate snaps of the tongue and firm smooches, not once letting her pussy recess.

Her whole body trembled. She started moaning in vibrations, as if she was on a roller coaster.

I felt her walls clench as I slid my fingers back out. I started taking off the rest of my clothes and she did the same. I got on top of her and stuffed a full mile of manhood in her wet pussy.

She sucked in a sharp breath. Then, with a gasp, she said, "You're big as fuck, Ray." Her fingernails dug into my back. "Nigga, you should've warned me. Oh my God!"

I bounced in and out of her pussy hard, losing all thoughts of the sensitivities of flesh and pain and how easily I had torn women's wombs in the past. *I want my nut, goddamnit.* Nothing else mattered—not her book, not a film script, not my girlfriend Natasha, nothing.

I rolled Phaedra's ass over onto her knees and guided my erection back into her sloppy wet pussy from behind. As soon as the head of my dick was fully buried within her—before I even had a chance to push my shaft all the way in—her warmness sent a magnetic charge through my blood-filled veins that tickled my testicles.

I pre-came.

I didn't have much longer. But I was still solid.

"Ohhh, yes, yes, yes!" Phaedra squealed as I pounded her doggystyle.

I filled her up with long, beefy thrusts of manpower, yanking in and out of her with primal lust. Her ass cheeks clapped against my waist.

"This is some good-ass muthafuckin' sweet shit!" I exclaimed, pounding her harder. "Bonafide A-1 country pussy right here, girl. This is that good shit, I swear, Phae."

She was moaning loudly. She snatched up a pillow and draped it over the back of her head, as if drowning out her screams would stop this dick from sliding.

"Phaedra!" I heard her sister shout. "Phaedra!"

I slowed down.

"Phaedra!"

I stopped. "Ay, Phae, yo sister is calling you." The writer didn't respond. I took the pillow off of her head and she looked back at me in a throe of confusion and disorientation.

"What happened?" she said.

"Yo sister is calling yo name." I pulled my saturated rod out of her. "It sounds important."

With a sigh, Phaedra climbed out of bed and stalked out of the bedroom naked. She went up to the bannister overlooking the foyer. I could still see her from the bed.

I was staring at her fat booty, stroking my shaft to keep myself hard.

"Patricia, why are you calling my name?"

"Somebody is at the door for you," I heard her sister say.

"Who is it?"

"The boy from the club. Lil Zoney."

Phaedra paused. She glanced back at me—I stopped stroking myself for some reason—and then she turned back toward her sister. "Tell him to wait in the living room," she said. "I'll be down in a minute."

Then she walked back in the room and got back in bed with me. Without a word of explanation, she started sucking my dick. Nasty, throat-touching bobs up and down. I couldn't believe it.

Chapter 6: Phaedra Hodges

I looked over at my digital clock on my nighstand just to confirm the time displayed on my laptop monitor (as if it were ever wrong). I couldn't believe it was 7:30 in the morning. I had been writing since 3 a.m., ever since Lil Zoney left my house.

I was sitting in the middle of my huge bed with my legs crossed under me, staring at the laptop, which sat before me on the same sheets I had just screwed Lil Zoney and Rayshawn on. This dirtiness I was resting on usually helped me to conjure up dirty thoughts. But for some reason my mind was drawing a blank. I stared at the blinking cursor on my screen, waiting for an idea—not a great idea, *any* idea— to pop in my head so I could finish writing this chapter for the sequel to *Petty*.

Etta James's "At Last" was playing softly on my stereo.

Then there was a knock on my bedroom door. As if I needed an interruption.

"Come in," I said.

My sister opened the door, wearing her morning robe tied over her wide hips. She yawned, patting her mouth with one hand and holding my door knob with the other. She seemed as if she was deciding whether or not she wanted to come in and bother me.

"You're up and at it early," she noted.

I shook my head no.

Her eyebrows shot up in surprise. "You haven't been to sleep yet?"

"No. I'm trying to finish the rest of this chapter up but I can't think of shit."

"You know why, don't you?"

"No, why?"

"Because you jinxed yourself." She came in and sat down on the edge of my bed. "You shouldn't have fucked Rayshawn. He's too much like Isaiah. You can't write because you're thinking of him."

"No, that's not true."

"You liar. It is too true."

As I thought about it, maybe Patricia was right. I would find myself playing out a fictional scene in my head, then my mind would drift to Rayshawn and his huge dick ramming in and out of me, giving me an intense pleasure I hadn't felt in a while. I had plenty of partners in the last few months, but nothing like Rayshawn. Lil Zoney didn't measure up to him in any way. That boy nutted quick and I sent him home.

"Rayshawn fucked you good, didn't he?" she asked.

I smiled and nodded yes. "He did indeed."

"I know he did. I seen parts of it on the monitor. You looked like you was going into convulsions when he started eating yo pussy."

I laughed at that and said, "You probably watched the whole session."

She wrinkled her nose, disgusted. "No, I didn't. I only look at you fuck when I have to." Then she got serious. "You're not inviting Rayshawn back over here, are you?"

I was the one wrinkling my nose now. "Heck no. He's a liar."

"What man isn't a liar?"

Thinking for a moment, I said, "Assad Blackwell isn't a liar. He's never lied to me in his life."

She rolled her eyes, and I laughed.

Assad Blackwell was a fictional character that appeared at the end of my bestseller *Petty*. He was going to have a leading role in the sequel I was currently writing. He was a divinely handsome brown-skinned alpha male that met Andrea—the protagonist based on me—after she was accused of murdering her husband. He overlooked her past and saw greatness in her—a greatness that her husband had refused to acknowledge. Assad never lied, he never misled her, and he was always a true gentleman.

"Let me know when you find an Assad in real life," said Patricia, heaving herself to her feet. "I think you should take Assad out of the sequel completely. He's so perfect that readers won't believe he's real. You had so much success with part one because it was based on real people."

"I'm not taking Assad out of my story. I already mentioned him in the first book."

"Yeah, at the end. Kill him off."

"No way."

"What if your editor asks you to take him out?"

With my thumb, I made a slicing gesture across my throat, indicating how I'd dispose of my editor if she tried to eject Assad, and Patricia rolled her eyes and headed back out of my room.

"I'm making breakfast for everybody," she told me over her shoulder. "Let me know if you want something other than the usual." She shut the door behind her.

I looked down at my laptop again, staring at the blinking cursor as if it were my worst enemy. I took a deep breath. I was at the scene where detectives had finally found my husband's mistress's body in the woods.

Flexing my fingers, I started typing:

The tail of Detective Huey Albitron's trench coat draped over dry grass as he squatted next to her corpse. The body hadn't been positively identified yet, but he knew—even through the pale blue hue of decomposition—he was staring at the missing exotic dancer Delana Cobbins. She had been missing for months. With an ink pen, he poked at the body's stiff hand, managing to get the writing end of the pen under her palm. He lifted it, paying close attention to the discoloration of her ring finger on her left hand. He turned to the crime scene photographer. "Make sure you get a close-up of this hand," he said.

I stopped there. I put Delana's real name in here, but that was just for my sake—the name would be changed to her fictional name, Robin Doherty, before I sent the final draft to my editor. I had a couple things to think about regarding this passage. For one, I wasn't sure if I wanted to have this detective wearing a trench coat because it seemed so cliché. Another thing—the more important question—was whether or not I should include Delana's missing engagement ring. It was too close to real life.

As I pondered over what to keep and what to omit, my subconscious mind started misbehaving again—Rayshawn had suddenly crept back into my thoughts. I was staring blankly at my screen as I imagined my legs wrapped around his torso, as he dug in and out of my pussy with a beast-like passion, as if we were the last of mankind.

I slapped my palms over my eyes. "Gotdammit, Rayshawn, get the fuck out of my head!"

Chapter 7: Rayshawn Meeks

"You did what?!" said Faheem Mathis, the director on set.

"I talked to Phaedra about her book," I said, as if I had done nothing wrong.

Faheem was an accomplished independent film director here in Atlanta, and his talents had been recognized by industry insiders all over the country. He was also my very good friend, despite how upset he was with me right now. He was brown-skinned, a little lighter complexion than myself, and he was thin—because he was a part-time athlete. He was wearing a small white T and some blue jeans, as he sat in the director's chair. It was lunch break. He had a Greek salad in his lap.

"Rayshawn, please tell me you didn't pursue her on your own," he said, forking some black olives and cucumbers in his mouth. "You better just be joking. Please don't tell me you approached Phaedra Hodges already."

"I did more than approach her, but look: I'm this close"—I pinched my thumb and forefinger together—"to getting her approval on the film."

"It's not just about her approval. She has a publisher that she has to go through too."

"I know. I didn't just start producing yesterday."

Faheem narrowed his eyes at me with his chin up, a look he gave when he felt that I had fucked something up. But this wasn't one of those times.

I found out about Phaedra Hodges and her New York Times bestselling book *Petty* through Faheem himself. He told me her book was a page-turner and it was going to be his next project if he could secure the movie rights. He had put off going to several different book signings of hers in other states but had made it a priority to attend this last one she had locally. Unfortunately, shooting this current drama-comedy film was taking up the bulk of his twenty-four hours and he couldn't make her local signing either.

So I decided to go.

Why is he mad at me for that?

"You didn't go after her because you liked her work," Faheem said knowingly.

I frowned, half smiling because he was right. "What are you tryna say?"

"I'm saying you're a whore. There's been plenty of writers, male and female, that you could've helped me pursue, but you picked Phaedra because you wanna fuck her."

"You think I'm that shallow?" But I couldn't stop smiling.

"Yes, you try to fuck every fine thing that comes on set. You ain't even read her book."

"So? But you have. And you said it was a good read; I trust yo judgement."

"Nah, you trust yo dick, nigga. You looked her up on the internet and yo dick said, 'Let's see what she talkin' 'bout, Rayshawn.' You need to cut that out, shawty. You got a good girl in Natasha, and you're just inviting bad karma on yourself."

Faheem was right about my tendency to slide in women with career goals in film. And sometimes I used my clout to persuade them to go to bed with me. But bad karma? No, bad karma only came in when you slept with a female and then backtracked on a prior deal. I still wanted to see Phaedra's book project come to fruition.

"Guess what?" I said.

He kept eating his salad, but looked at me with interested eyes.

"I fucked her last night, into this morning," I confessed.

He smiled, then looked down at his salad and stirred it up with his fork. "Quit lying. You ain't fucked shit. That woman is bad and accomplished. What she need to fuck you for?"

"That's the thing," I said, getting excited. "I didn't even plan to fuck her yet. I thought I wouldn't be able to get her panties until after we signed some paperwork. But she invited me in her home. Then up to her room."

"Where she live at then?"

"Tuxedo Park."

He dropped his fork and scowled at me. It wasn't a game anymore. "You really fucked Phaedra Hodges?"

"Yes, sir. With hardly no effort, other than my usual trademark persistence. She's a freak too."

"Of course she is. You would know that if you read her novel. In the second half of the book there's a sex scene where the protagonist sleeps with her husband and his mistress at the same time. Then both her husband and the mistress beat her ass bloody with a leather belt. That's what sent her over the edge. And that's the scene she's famous for." He stirs his salad again, but now he seems disinterested in it. He sets it to the side and plants his elbows on the thin wood arms of his director's chair. He fixes me with a stern look. "Leave her alone," he tells me. "You got what you wanted. You got the pussy. But stop trying to put together a deal. I don't want you to fuck this up."

"What makes you think I'll fuck it up? Me and her have something going."

"I don't care. I'm really excited about bringing her book to life. Not only do I think it's lucrative, but I like her story and the way it's written. She's a survivor. Projects like hers don't come around often and I don't want to lose it."

"You won't. My job as a producer is to secure scripts. Let me handle this one. That's yo problem—you keep trying to do every aspect of the film process yo'self. You hired me for shit like this."

"No, I hired you because you're my boy and I got tired of you asking me for money, so I put you to work."

I placed my right hand over my heart, wincing in fake pain. "That's cold, shawty."

"I don't care."

Actors and actresses, cameramen and women along with the lighting crews, started to make their way back on set. Faheem got out of his seat and walked over to an actress that was starring in the next scene. I watched him walk away—without saying another word to me.

I pulled my phone out of my pocket and looked at my text messages. I had sent Phaedra a text about a half hour ago, asking her when we could have another meeting, a more formal meeting.

She hadn't replied yet.

"Maybe I did fuck the deal up," I said to myself, sighing. "Damn, Rayshawn, did you not lay the pipe good enough?"

Chapter 8: Rayshawn Meeks

It had been two weeks since I slept with Phaedra Hodges. And in that two weeks I had been calling and texting her and leaving emails, asking for a follow-up visit. I hadn't gotten any type of reply from any of my means of communication.

Is she curbing me? Was Faheem right? Did I fuck up the deal?

To make sure Phaedra knew I wasn't trying to get in touch with her merely for more sex, I laid out a detailed plan for her novel in an email—I listed popular screenwriters she could collaborate with, potential actors and actresses that she'd mentioned that I could pull onboard, and I even gave her a link to Faheem Mathis's Wikipedia page.

And as of yet, I hadn't heard back.

Ever since I was a hardheaded child, I hated being told no. Faheem told me once that my personality—my dogged perseverance and my manipulative way with words—made me a great producer but a horrible person to work with day to day. I took it as his style of saying he loved me. And also that Phaedra wasn't avoiding ya boy; she was just having a hard time accepting my personality.

As I drove through Tuxedo Park on my way to her house—in a rented Maserati Ghibli paid for by the studio—I flipped down my visor and looked at my reflection in the mini-mirror. Licking my lips, I smiled at myself. "How can any woman say no to you, Rayshawn? You got the looks, you got the game, you got the money ..." I flipped the mirror up as Phaedra's mega-home came into view. "... and you got the balls."

I parked in front of the huge house, got out and walked up the steps onto the front porch. I knocked on the front door with the gold-plated door knocker.

I waited a full minute, and after no one came, I knocked again. With my knuckles this time.

As I continued to wait, I glanced over my shoulder at the Porsche Panamera parked in front of my Maserati. "She's home," I said to myself. "Somebody's home, gotdammit."

I gave the door a few more raps, then took a few steps back to see if I could look in a window.

Every curtain on the first level was closed.

I walked up to the door again—this time I tried the knob.

I turned it and it opened.

"Hello?" I called into the house with half my body inside. No response but my own soft echo. "Hello? It's me, Rayshawn Meeks, the producer. Anybody home?"

"Help me!"

The sudden cry scared me, made me flinch. It was loud but muffled, as if the scream came from behind a door.

I walked all the way in, craning my neck to peer down the hallway. I left the front door cracked just in case I needed to turn and run out.

"Hello? Phaedra? You okay?"

As I took cautious steps further into the home, I tried to assess the scream and determine how dire it sounded. I couldn't tell if it was a man or a woman's voice. It could have been another one of Phaedra's man friends, them playing some kind of kinky game. But my gut was telling me the cry for help was real.

"Phaedra?" I said, looking around as I passed the living room and then the kitchen, where someone left the light on. "Phaedra, you okay girl?"

At the end of the hallway there was a door. It looked slightly ajar. The scream sounded like it would have come from behind this door. Not upstairs, not anywhere else but behind this door.

I think.

As I put my hand on the knob—*creeaak!*—it suddenly squeaked all the way open and I jumped back. Patricia West, Phaedra's big sister, emerged. She sort of squeezed out the door as if she didn't want me to see what was behind it. She swiftly shut it closed.

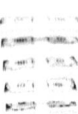

But before she did I got a glimpse of a set of stairs leading downward—to the basement, I presumed.

"What the hell are you doing in my house?!" she snapped on me. Then she pushed me backwards.

"I heard somebody scream for help."

"You're a damn lie!"

"No, I'm not. I know what I heard. What do you think I'm doing in here? You think I just walk in people's houses? I came in to help."

"You heard the TV upstairs, not nobody yelling help."

I glanced up at the ceiling, waiting for sounds that would indicate a television show or a commercial was playing. I heard nothing. It was deathly quiet in this mansion.

"And you wouldn't have heard a damn thing," she added, "if you didn't illegally open my front door and stick yo big-ass head inside."

"How'd you see me open the door? Where were you?"

"Now you're asking too many questions." She pushed me again. "Get out!"

"No, I'm not leaving until I talk to Phaedra," I said adamantly, as I glanced behind her at the basement door again. "Where is she? She hasn't been returning my calls, my texts, or my emails. I need to know that she's okay."

"She's fine. Get the fuck out before I call the police."

"Phaedra!" I hollered.

"She's not here!"

"Where is she?"

"She's in another state. She's on her book tour." Patricia grabbed me by my arms and turned me around, then she started pushing against the middle of my back, forcing me to walk down the hallway toward the front door.

I threw a remark over my shoulder: "That don't explain why she's not getting back with me."

"She doesn't like you, Rayshawn. And neither do I."

"What did I do wrong?" I asked.

It can't be my dick game, I knew. She was loving how I was putting it down. Moaning, screaming, clawing my back. You can fake a good time, but you *can't* fake all that cum that was running out of her.

"Don't take it personal," Patricia said, still pushing me out. I was having trouble keeping my footing. Close to the front door, she stopped shoving and walked around me. She pulled open the front door—which I had left cracked—and she waved her hand outside. She was giving me a chance to walk out on my own first. Because she was tired. "Bon voyage, Rayshawn," she panted.

"What do you mean don't take it personal?" I asked, offended. "How am I supposed to take it?"

"Phaedra fucks men all the time and never calls them again. It's not you. She just needs variety to keep fresh sex scenes pouring through her novels."

"That's all fine and dandy. My ego ain't hurt," I lied. "I'm just trying to talk to her about her book becoming a movie."

"She's had plenty of people approach her about a movie. She's not interested."

"Let her tell me that to my face."

"Don't make me go get my knife," she said tiredly, as if the walk to fetch her weapon was the hard part—and killing me easy.

Digging in my back pocket, I pulled out my wallet and flipped it open expertly. I plucked out a business card and held it out to her.

She didn't even look at it. She was just staring me in the eyes, as if I should have known she wouldn't take the card.

"Please?" I said.

"She already has your number if she wanted to use it."

"This isn't my business card," I informed her. "This is Faheem Mathis's business card. He's a world-famous director, and he's from right here in Atlanta, Georgia. If Phaedra feels like she doesn't want to do business with me, tell her to at least give him a call."

Patricia finally took the card, using it in conjunction with her hand to make a scooping motion out the door. "Now bye. Off you go. Don't let the door hit ya where the Good Lord split ya."

I gave her a kind smile and walked out the house, trotting down the porch steps as she slammed the door behind me.

Starting up the Maserati and driving away, I watched Phaedra's mansion gradually shrink in my rearview mirror. And long after I left Tuxedo Park, I still couldn't wrap my head around that scream I heard.

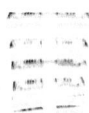

Chapter 9: Rayshawn Meeks

The bell above the door dinged as I walked into the barbershop on Peters Street. I said hi to a few of the stylists and took a seat in Rocc's chair, after giving him some dap and a brotherly half hug. He was an ex-con turned barber, one of the most popular in the city.

"Fashion-forward as always," said Rocc with a smile, referring to my checkered grey Tom Ford sport jacket. It was slim fit, fastened at my stomach with one black button. And I had a silver clip attached to my tie today.

"I'm trying to top it off with a sharp haircut," I replied.

"Your usual?"

"Yes, sir. Fade me up."

He snapped his black cape and let it fall across me gracefully, as he clipped the cape's collar at the nape of my neck. My phone buzzed and I dug it out from underneath the cape to check the notification. I was hoping it was a text or email from Phaedra Hodges, but it wasn't; it was just a social media comment. A female follower put: "Do the damn thang then," on a mirror selfie I posted this morning in this sport jacket.

. *Dammit, Phaedra,* I cursed silently. *Where the fuck are you? Hit me back so we can work, baby girl.*

"Hi, Rayshawn," Lanivia, a hair stylist, said to me in an exaggerated cadence, as if she was a fan of mine.

I thought I already said hi to everybody when I walked in here, but apparently not.

"Hey, Lanivia, how you doing today?" I said over the buzz of Rocc's clippers.

"Mmm," she uttered with a slight shoulder shrug, and I had no idea what that meant. But I knew it wasn't good.

Me and Lanivia had history. She was a fine sista with a curvy body, and she knew how to accentuate her figure with the right outfits. She had style, which was what attracted me to her. Right now she was playing in a customer's hair, fluffing it with her fingers. Even as she stood behind the chair that her client was sitting in, you could see her big hips poking out on either side.

Her ass was mega fat and shapely, the jiggly authentic kind too. A few months back I was behind it, ramming my dick in her lubricated asshole as if I had a point to prove. Her chocolate skin was silky with sweat; it made her whole backside glow brilliantly under the starlit ceiling of the rented Rolls-Royce we were in. She let me fuck because I promised her a part in an upcoming movie I was piecing together casting-wise. She let me do so much nasty shit to her—ass-to-mouth, twice, and I came in her face and she rubbed it in and let it crust over—that you would've thought I was giving her the starring role in *Hidden Figures.*

The upcoming movie I promised her was actually the one me and Faheem were currently working on now. And as of yet I hadn't given Lanivia a call. And I didn't plan to.

Rocc responded to Lanivia's "Mmm" comment with: "Uh-oh, here we go. She's about to get started."

A couple people laughed.

"No, I'm not," she said. Then she smacked her lips. "I just want to ask the man a question."

I kept my lips tight as Rocc lined up my mustache.

"Where's my script for my role?" Lanivia threw at me. "You didn't think I forgot, did you?"

"Is that why you ain't been in my chair in a minute?" Rocc instigated. "You been avoiding my co-worker?"

I *had* been avoiding her. My last few haircuts were at a shop off Cascade Road. I only stopped in here because it was closer to a scene that Faheem was shooting on location. However, I wanted to turn and look at Rocc and say, *Nigga, didn't you learn some kind of prison code against egging on drama?*

Instead, partly because Rocc was still buzzing at my mustache and my chin hairs, I could only murmur, "Nah."

Everyone laughed.

Except Lanivia. "I don't find nothing funny," she said. "I thought all a man had was his balls and his word."

"Rayshawn ain't got neither," Rocc cracked.

More laughter.

"I got something coming up for you," I said to Lanivia. "As soon as we get our next movie rolling, you're a shoo-in."

"I heard Faheem already got a movie rolling," she said knowingly. "Ain't he filming something right around the corner from here?"

Fuck, I thought. *This bitch know everything. I hate social media sometimes.*

Quick on my feet, I said, "I'm not working with him on this movie."

Rocc said, "The lie detector determined: that was a lie."

He got more laughs. I almost laughed myself.

"I know he's lying," Lanivia said, sucking her teeth. "Rocc, you ain't telling me nothing I don't know. Him and Faheem are like brothers. Yall work on every movie together, Rayshawn. You act like I can't read movie credits."

"Seriously, Lanivia. You won't see my name on the credits of this movie Faheem got popping right now," I stated. "I'm in no way involved." I was dishing out pure bullshit. My name would be in the credits in bold letters. But by the time the movie was actually released, I'd have a whole new pile of shit to shovel at her. "This film he's doing now is a drama comedy. I don't fuck with those fa-real. You don't wanna be in a funny movie anyway. You're more of a serious actor."

She smiled. "I am?"

"Yeah. This next movie we're teaming up on is more your speed."

"What's the name of it?"

"It's called *Petty*. It's based on a novel by—"

"Phaedra Hodges!" she finished for me excitedly.

I was surprised she knew the author's name. "You read?" I said.

A few giggles spread through the shop.

Lanivia scowled at me. "Yes I read, nigga. I don't read as much as I should but I read that book."

"I read it too," said the lady in Lanivia's chair. She was a light-skinned woman who looked to be in her late forties, with lots of brittle hair and barely-noticeable freckles dotting her cheeks and nose. "It was *gooood*. One of the best books I read this year."

"I downloaded it on e-book," said another girl who was waiting to be seen. "But I haven't started reading it yet. I heard it was a page-turner."

"It is," said the freckled client. "I don't wanna give away the whole story, but there's a scene where she's in the bed with her husband and his mistress getting it on and—"

"The husband yanks her ass on the floor!" Lanivia chimes in with excitement.

Her client was just as excited. "Yes! And then he started beating her ass with the belt."

"Then he gave the belt to his mistress and she beat her ass too! Hell no, that couldn't be me."

"The whole thing was a part of the husband and the mistress's kinky little game."

The girl who was still waiting to be seen didn't seem bothered by the spoiler. "Didn't the author get away with murdering her husband and his mistress in real life?"

"They still haven't found the bodies," said the freckled woman. "And they didn't have enough evidence to take her to trial. In the book, she claims that another one of her husband's side chicks killed them. But in real life everybody knows she's the one that did it."

This was news to me. I had no idea that Phaedra's fans thought she was a murderer. No wonder Faheem wanted this film so bad—Phaedra's story was sensational.

I gotta get Phaedra to say yes to us, I thought.

"It took a minute for her to get paid from the life insurance," Lanivia began, "because of the murder investigation. But after that check came, I know she was living fat, baby. Yo go Phaedra."

"Yep," the freckled woman agreed. "But she was already living fat before the insurance money came, and before the book deal. Her husband was a real estate tycoon, and she was doing pretty well in real estate herself. That's how she and her husband met; they were on opposite ends of trying to close a house. Phaedra was an agent for the seller, and her husband was an agent for the buyer. They had a mansion together in Tuxedo Park."

Lanivia pointed a hot comb at me. "You better get me the leading role of Phaedra Hodges. You hear me, nigga?"

"All I can do is get you the audition," I told her. "You're on your own from there."

After Rocc finished getting me right, I paid him cash and then gave him dap and another half hug. On my way out the shop, I was looking down at my phone, thumbing in another text to the infamous Phaedra Hodges.

Chapter 10: Phaedra Hodges

The waiter pulled my chair out and I sat down, swinging my legs under the table. Then he helped me scoot the seat in.

"Thank you," I said to him with a kind smile, despite my reason for being here.

"You're welcome, Ms. Hodges. Can I start you off with a drink?"

"A bulldog gin, please."

"Coming right up, ma'am."

I was at an upscale steakhouse off Peachtree Street. In a long, ruffled-back blazer over a seamless cami—with a pair of strappy high heels and my hair pinned up—I looked like I was here to meet the man of my dreams. Instead, I was here to dismiss a playboy film producer. I always aimed to dress attractive and sexy—and on club nights, slutty and porny—because Isaiah had always had say-so over what I wore out. The only time he let me show some skin above the knee was when I was in public with him.

So my attire tonight wasn't for Rayshawn. It was for me.

Looking up from my menu, I watched Rayshawn approach. He was wearing a sharp gray suit—Tom Ford, I guessed—with an eye-popping gold Rolex on his wrist. He casted a self-assured smile that made my skin crawl, because it reminded me of my ex-husband. Isaiah would smile at me the same way whenever I picked him up from the airport, after one of his weekend getaways with Delana Cobbins—getaways he thought I didn't know about.

"Nice to see you again," Rayshawn said, coming over to my side of the table.

Reluctantly, I got up and gave him a hug. He kissed me on the cheek, then we sat back down. I sneakily stared across the table at him as he opened up his menu; I tried to tell myself that he wasn't as handsome as I initially thought—but he was.

"Okay," he said, then rubbed his hands together with greedy intent. "I don't know where to start. I'm too excited."

"You shouldn't be," I said.

His expression sunk. "Why not?"

"Because this is the last time you'll be seeing me."

"I don't understand." He set his menu down. "I thought we were here to talk about our plans for *Petty* the movie."

"Why would I discuss plans like that with a burglar?"

He looked struck. The he laughed a little after he realized what I was talking about.

The waiter came back with my gin and then he asked Rayshawn what he would like to drink. He said gin too, and I had no idea if he was copying me or if he really enjoyed gin.

Before the waiter even left, Rayshawn said, "How am I a burglar? I didn't take nothing out of your house."

I waited until the waiter was gone before I replied: "Patricia told me you walked in my house on your own free will. That's a crime. That's breaking and entering."

"No, it would've been a crime if I *didn't* go in. I thought I heard somebody scream for help."

I blanched. Patricia informed me that Rayshawn walked in the house uninvited but she conveniently left out the part about the scream for help. *That bitch. What the fuck was she doing down there?*

"I don't care what you heard," I told him, hoping he didn't catch my surprise.

"If that's why you're choosing not to work with me, then I sincerely apologize. I won't let it happen again."

"It's not just that."

He made a frightened face. "Damn, what else is it?"

"You're a liar."

"What did I lie about, Phaedra?

"You said you read my book."

"I did read it."

83

"Okay," I said in a challenging tone. I crossed my arms on the table. "What did the husband and his mistress do to the wife that caused her to snap?"

"Easy one," he said quickly. "They beat her with a belt."

I was actually surprised that he knew that. But not too surprised since that was one of the most talked about scenes on all the book blogs.

"You're right," I said, "that was an easy one. But not this next one: What weapon did the killer use to murder the husband and the wife?"

He hesitated. "A gun."

"Wrong."

"No, wait. I'm thinking of a different book. The killer used a knife."

"Wrong."

"A baseball bat."

I leaned forward. "*Wrong.*"

"A frying pan?" he asked me.

I laughed at him derisively. "You didn't read shit."

He sighed. "Okay, I didn't read your book. But that doesn't mean I'm not serious about the project. My life is just too busy to sit down and read a book cover to cover."

"But you weren't too busy to cheat on your girlfriend Natasha with me."

His eyes went wide. "Holy shit, shawty! What'd you do, send a private investigator after me?"

"No, you're not that important. That information was given to me voluntarily from your friend Faheem Mathis."

His shock intensified, then he seemed severely bothered by my insight. "If that ain't fuck boy shit, then I don't know what is. Faheem snitched?"

"You left his number with Patricia so I gave him a call to see how legit you were," I said while grinning. "He told me a lot of interesting things about you. Natasha was just one of 'em."

"How are you gon' judge me by my sex life, when you had a little thug nigga named Lil Zoney waiting downstairs for his turn to fuck while I was still fucking you?"

"It's not about sex, Rayshawn. I love sex. It's about honesty."

"Faheem's the one who told you I didn't read yo book?"

"No, I already knew that."

"How?"

"The night I invited you to my room. I asked you did you know what cheater's paranoia was. You said no. If you read *Petty*, you would've known that I mentioned cheater's paranoia throughout the whole book."

He started chewing on the inside of his lip. "So what now? You gon' work with Faheem directly?"

"I haven't decided yet. He seems like a nice, honest guy, but so did you. He did tell me that if I agreed to work with him, he'd make sure you weren't involved in the project."

"That son of a bitch."

The waiter returned with Rayshawn's gin and asked if we were ready to order our meals. Rayshawn didn't answer; he had pulled out his cell phone and was now texting somebody. Faheem, I was sure.

I smiled at the waiter cheerfully. "Yes, sir, I'm ready. And whatever he orders"—I pointed at Rayshawn—"make sure it has little to no salt. He's feeling salty enough as it is."

Chapter 11: Rayshawn Meeks

I rented a red bicycle for ten dollars from a young kid who was about to hit the Suwanee Greenway Trail in Pierce Park. In a full suit—blazer, long-sleeve button-up shirt, slacks and loafers—I climbed on the bike and started pedaling along the trail, deep into the forest comprised of Georgia's natural wetlands. It had been ages since I rode a bicycle. I didn't know how well my legs would do, but I was holding up. And the cool breeze whipping against my face was refreshing.

I pedaled until I caught up with Faheem Mathis, who was on foot, jogging along the trail in basketball shorts and Asics running shoes. His chiseled upper body glistened with sweat.

"Hey, traitor," I said as I pedaled next to him.

He looked over at me with surprise, still jogging. Then he smiled. I noticed he had Bluetooth earbuds in his ear so he didn't hear my comment. He took them out one by one and jogged with them in his fist.

"Rayshawn, what in the Sam Hill are you doing on a bike in a suit?" Faheem panted as he talked. He was probably on his fourth mile by now.

"I came to look my enemy in the face," I said.

"Enemy?"

"Yeah, you told Phaedra not to fuck with me, didn't you?"

He grinned. "She finally answered your calls?"

"She agreed to dinner and broke the news to me. She told me you told her all about Natasha and the fact that I didn't read her book. Is that the type of games we're playing now?"

"You started playing this game first. You had no business approaching her. She was my project."

"Nigga, I was helping you because you were too busy!"

"No, you were helping yourself because Phaedra is gorgeous and you wanted some pussy."

I gripped my handlebars tight as we crossed a wooden boardwalk. My tires vibrated over the planks. Other than that, this trail's terrain was reasonably bike-friendly.

"You're lucky I got her to agree to a sit down with me this weekend," he added.

"You had to throw me under the bus to make that happen?" I asked.

"Yes, I did. She told me she was turned off by you and your lies, that you reminded her too much of her husband, so I had to let her know that I agreed with her description of you. I told her I didn't like you either. I had to. Because we were able to bond over that. She opened up to me."

"So you're really not gonna let me on set when yall start her movie?"

"I don't know, Rayshawn." He was panting harder. Talking and jogging was making him more winded. "We'll see if she has a change of heart when the time comes."

"So she really hates me, huh?"

He chuckled. "You sound sad. You still wanna fuck, don't you?"

"Hell yeah. Her pussy was good as fuck."

"You need to move on, shawty."

Then Faheem suddenly broke out into a sprint. To catch up, I stood up off my seat and pressed down hard on the pedal.

Snap!—the chain popped. I was terrified as the front handlebars zig-zagged and my left foot slid off the pedal, which rotated down and around in a flash, stabbing into my Achilles' heel. I let out a painful wail but managed to get both feet planted on the ground before I lost my balance.

With the broken bike poised between my legs, I stared down the curve of the Suwanee Greenway Trail. Faheem Mathis was long gone.

Chapter 12: Phaedra Hodges

I was still looking in the full-length mirror in my bedroom when the doorbell rang. I adjusted the strapless top of my little black dress, causing my big brown breasts to wobble, then I ran my hands along the curves of my hips, smoothing out the wrinkles in the polyester. My make-up was shining, my lips were saturated with an eye-popping purple, and if my stilettos were any steeper I'd fall forward with every step.

A recurring thought came to me: Isaiah would've never approved of this. He would've dragged me back upstairs by my arm—or my hair, depending on his temperament—and ripped this dress off of me and shredded it up. Then dared me to cry.

"He's here!" Patricia called from downstairs. "Do you want me to let him in?"

"No!" I shouted back. "Is the table ready?"

"Not yet. All I have to do is—"

"Get the damn table ready! I'll get the door!"

I probably shouted a little louder than I had to but I was still upset that she didn't tell me about the scream for help. When I confronted her about it, she said that Rayshawn believed her when she said the scream was just a figment of his imagination—but that wasn't the point. If Rayshawn heard a scream, that meant the basement door had been left open. And we agreed to never leave the basement door open.

She was being careless.

Sighing, I turned slightly to check my side profile in the mirror. My tummy was tight, my chest was out, and my butt had southern magnitude. Not bad for 35.

I was hurrying down the staircase when my guest knocked again.

"Coming!" I said expectantly.

I opened the front door and smiled at Faheem Mathis standing on my porch. "*Hello,*" I said with a flirty drawl.

The smile he gave me was infectious. "Hello, Ms. Hodges."

"Don't do that," I said, and it made his smile widen. "You better call me Phaedra."

"Sorry, Phaedra. You look great."

"Thank you. You don't look too bad yourself. Come on in?"

A natural oceanic cologne wafted from Faheem as he walked into my house and I shut the door behind him. He had his hands stuffed in a pair of tight denim jeans, with a pair of white and navy blue Air Jordans on his feet. His white T-shirt was a chest-hugger, and boy was his chest big! His biceps were huge too, but overall he was slim and toned. Needless to say, he was athletic—a far cry from Rayshawn's jiggly tummy.

"I feel underdressed," he said, eyeing my skimpy outfit.

"Don't. I'm a habitual overdresser. I dress up to go to the grocery store. I dress up at the laundromat. I dress up at home sometimes, just to write."

He nodded and looked around my house, his head making a big arc from right to left. My ceilings were immensely high and vaulted. "This is really-really nice, Phaedra. Wow."

"Thank you."

"What's that smell? It smells good as hell." He rubbed his flat stomach.

"My sister cooked a nice meal for us. If she can't do nothing else, that bitch can cook. May I?"

He seemed puzzled by my question until he saw my hand. "Oh," he said, and interlaced his fingers in mine.

We started walking to the kitchen, hand in hand.

I didn't have to grab his hand. In fact, I couldn't ever remember doing this before, leading a man by the hand as if we were a young couple in love. But I felt compelled to touch him, to feel his strength, to feel that skin to skin

intimacy, and this was the quickest and subtlest way to do that without scaring him off.

"Faheem, this is Patricia. Patricia, this is Faheem. He's the film director I was telling you about," I said as we entered the kitchen.

I held on to Faheem's hand a little longer than I should have, as he started toward Patricia. He had to look back at me with a let-my-hand-go sort of smile. Then he went around the island and gave Patricia a hug and a kiss on the cheek.

I haven't even gotten a hug and a kiss yet, I complained silently.

"Nice to meet you," Faheem said to her.

Patricia actually gave him a welcoming smile. "Nice to meet you too, Faheem."

"I was just telling Phaedra how good it smelled when I walked in the house. I can't wait to try you out."

Patricia looked at me while pointing at Faheem. "I like this one."

We all shared a laugh, and I directed Faheem to the dining room, holding his hand again.

Patricia had cooked a giant family-style dinner—spinach lasagna, Moroccan-spiced chicken, garlic potatoes, grilled vegetables and textured corn pudding. A bottle of red wine sat in the middle of the table. I didn't give Faheem an option to choose a non-alcoholic beverage. I had instructed Patricia to make sure his glass stayed full.

Me and Faheem sat next to each other facing the kitchen, our backs to the rear of the house where the basement door was. Patricia slowly poured his first glass and asked him, "So you wanna turn my sister's book into a movie too, huh?"

"Too?" he questioned. "I take that to mean she's had a lot of offers."

"A few," said Patricia. "But she hasn't been approached by anybody that has convinced her that they'd do a good job bringing her book to life."

Faheem glanced over at me and I nodded my head in agreement with my sister.

Patricia took her seat across from us. "It's always con games," she continued. "People see a bestselling book and just wanna make a quick buck off her. Nobody has been as passionate about her work as she is. Half the folks that come at her haven't even read her book. Case in point: your friend, Rayshawn Meeks."

"I'm not Rayshawn Meeks," said Faheem. "And I say that proudly."

I chuckled. "So you're saying you've actually read the book?"

Faheem nodded yes as he forked a mound of garlic potatoes in his mouth. He chewed, swallowed, then licked

his lips—top and bottom. He even rolled his lips in, savoring the taste. He was tearing Patricia's cooking up.

"Okay," I began. "Name one character besides the main character. And you can't name her husband either because it's listed on the back of the book."

"Robin Doherty," he said. "She's the mistress."

"Name another one," I said.

"Detective Huey Albitron. He's hell-bent on proving that you're—I'm sorry, proving that the protagonist Andrea Howard—is guilty of killing her husband and his mistress."

Patricia's turn: "Okay. Who turned out to be the killer in the end?"

"It was another one of the husband's side chicks," Faheem answered correctly. "Tracy Pritchard."

"Good job," I said. "Now for the bonus question. This one will make or break you." I turned to him, draping my elbow over the back of my own chair. "What was the term cheater's paranoia a reference to in the book?"

Faheem took a sip of his wine. Confidently, he said, "Cheater's paranoia was what Andrea diagnosed her husband with. He constantly cheated on her, so much so that it became ingrained in his mind that everyone in every relationship cheated. And because of his mindset—because of the delusions derived from his own guilt—he accused Andrea of being unfaithful too. And he beat her up. Most of his physical violence came because he couldn't catch her in the act. He couldn't grasp the logic that she simply wasn't cheating. His thoughts were, 'I'm a fucked up, poor excuse of a man. Who wouldn't cheat on me? She has to be cheating.''

Impressed, I looked over at Patricia, who was smiling in delight.

"He read it," she affirmed.

"Bravo," I said.

"I wasn't finished explaining the term," he stated.

"Oh." I looked at Patricia again; I made an "oops" face. And she was studying Faheem with new, deep interest. "Go ahead," I said.

"This wasn't explicitly stated in the novel, but I also think Andrea herself was suffering from cheater's paranoia," he told us. "She wasn't cheating physically, per se, but she was in and out of other relationships mentally. I'm talking about the short erotic stories that Andrea wrote. They were full of vivid sex. Not just your ordinary sex either. She got down and dirty—lesbian stuff, group sex, multiple men with one girl, voyeurism. You name it, she imagined it and brought it to life on paper."

I was held captive as he continued.

"I think Andrea loved the characters she was writing about more than she loved her husband. Which, to me, is understandable," he said, touching his chest with all five fingers of his left hand. "But to her, she was just as unfaithful as her husband. She would read her own sex scenes and

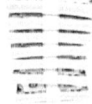

masturbate to them, then feel guilty afterwards. I think that's why she tolerated her husband's mistresses. And I think that's why she agreed to the ménage à trois with Robin Doherty. It was a combination of guilt, curiosity, and cheater's paranoia. Except her paranoia was valid."

Me and Patricia gave Faheem a sitting ovation. Patricia was fast-clapping, always trying to outdo somebody.

"Damn good job," said Patricia.

"Thank you."

"I've read a lot of reviews of my work," I said, "and I've never seen or heard anybody relate cheater's paranoia to Andrea."

"So I was accurate?" he asked.

"Yes. When I re-read my first short story—"

Patricia suddenly cleared her throat and stood up, reaching for the bottle of wine. She re-filled Faheem's glass.

I looked at her, then realized my mistake. "Oh, when *she* ... When Andrea re-read her first erotic story from years ago, from high school, her own writing was foreign to her. She vaguely remembered writing it, and thus the characters felt brand new. She was married to Isaiah—"

Again, Patricia cleared her throat.

I sighed, irritated. I kept getting real names mixed up with fictional ones. "Andrea was married to Shamar at the time she found the story at her mother's house. She played with herself after reading it, and she climaxed. From that point on, her love of writing was re-born. She started to feel less and less of an inadequate wife and gained confidence from the male characters she created is her stories. She fell in love with the heroes. The only bad part was men like the ones she was writing about don't exist in real life."

Faheem shook his head. He disagreed. "How would she know that men like that don't really exist? She got married to a loser at a young age. There *are* men out there that know how to treat a woman right."

I blinked. "You think so?"

"I know so."

Faheem stared at me for a moment, and I stared back, wanting to believe that his words were true. I knew it was just my imagination, but it seemed as if Faheem's eyes were telling me, *I'm your Assad Blackwell.*

"Sorry to interrupt you guys' staring contest," said Patricia, "but I have to go feed the dog." She stood up and started scooping spoonfuls of spinach lasagna onto a new clean plate.

"Yall feed yall dog lasagna?" Faheem asked.

"Yep," Patricia answered with a cavalier attitude. "Beggars can't be choosy."

I gave her a long, mean look as she left the table.

Just me and Faheem now, we talked about the business of converting my book to film and about the book's underground success prior to reaching bestseller status.

Faheem told me that he had one goal in mind when it came to the portrayal of Andrea Howard on screen—he wanted the world to feel her struggle. By the end of the film, he wanted viewers to wish she had killed her own husband, to wish the second side chick wasn't the murderer, because the side chick deserved to be murdered too. He even proposed changing the ending, where Andrea actually did commit the crime of killing her husband.

"No," I said quickly.

"Why not?"

I hesitated.

"Because people still think you killed him?" he said. "You don't wanna get people that riled up?"

"Exactly."

We each took a bite of our food.

Then I wiped my mouth with a napkin. "Would you like to come upstairs to my room?" I asked him.

"Sure. What's up there?"

"I wanna show you this story I've been working on."

"Cool. What's this one about?"

"The science behind what makes women cum."

His eyes bulged out.

Chapter 13: Faheem Mathis

Phaedra took me by the hand again. I barely had a chance to wipe my mouth as she led me out of her dining room.

"So it's an erotic story?" I asked nervously.

We were heading up her staircase now. I was staring at her butt as it took on new curve-defining shape with each step upward. I thought of what Rayshawn told me about how he slept with Phaedra on the first night ...

Is that about to happen to me too?

Or am I wishful-thinking?

"As a whole it's not erotic," she said. "It's just a scene I'm working on. It's a sex scene."

Once in her room she let my hand go and kicked off her stilettos, then she crawled into her bed. As she crawled to the center of it, her amazing rear end and the soles of her bare feet were facing me. I wanted to follow behind her. My dick was awakening. I could feel it beginning to swell.

Damn, she's sexy.

I thought she was about to grab her laptop off of her nightstand, but she didn't. She simply turned over and faced me, staring at me as if I was supposed to know what to do.

I was standing near her door with my hands in my jean pockets.

"Where's the story?" I asked her.

"That's the thing," she said. "I need help creating it."

Slowly, she bent her knee toward her, as she rested back on her elbows. If she were to turn her knee outward, I would've been able to see directly between her legs. Instead, she turned it in, crossing it over her other leg; this sight was no less stunning, for her dress slid up a tad, showing more of her bare thigh than a man was supposed to see. Actually, she was showing more than just thigh—her bare buttocks was exposed, the curve of it at least.

My heart started beating fast. *Is this really about to happen?!*

"The main male character's name is Assad Blackwell," she continued. "He's like the hero of the story. He comes and starts to change Andrea's heart about men. He tells her he's nothing like her husband. In this scene, Andrea is letting Assad touch her for the first time."

"And you want them to have sex?" I asked.

"Yes. But I just don't know how to start it, from a man's point of view."

"Well, if I was Assad, I would most definitely take it slow with her. Since her husband used to beat her routinely, he would have to be gentle with her."

"How?"

"Maybe, uh ..."

My voice trailed off when she slowly turned her knee outward—and I could see directly between her legs. The lights from the ceiling fan eliminated any shadow; her gaping moist pussy and all of its pinkness was glowing bright.

"He might start with ... uh ... an uh ... a simple kiss," I said, my words leaving me. "He'd probably just kiss her."

"Where? I'm a writer, I need details."

Because my mouth was suddenly dry, I merely pointed to the side of my own neck. "Maybe right here."

"Show me."

Her knee went in again, and her pink flower disappeared. But just when my breath started to come back, she let her knee sway back out. *Pussy!* Then in. Gone. Then out again. *Pussy!*

She's flashing me ... she's teasing me ...

"Show me," she repeated. "Faheem, show me your vision of Assad."

"Show you?"

"Yes. Show me. C'mere." She threw her chin to the side, an added gesture for me to come to her.

I walked over to the foot of the bed.

"Take your shoes off," she told me.

I loosened the laces of my Jordans and kicked them off, then climbed in bed with her.

"Show me," she whispered seductively, closing her eyes and turning her head, which exposed her smooth brown neck.

I leaned in and kissed her just below her ear, softly. "Maybe somethin' like that," I whispered. "Or maybe even ..." I nibbled on her earlobe. "You think your readers will like that?"

"I need more," she said, her eyes still closed. "What else?"

I licked my lips. "Let me see ... So many beautiful places to start ..."

I turned her chin toward me and kissed her deeply on the lips. Passionately I sucked on her top lip, then bottom, as I laid her flat on her back. I tugged on the chest of her strapless dress, freeing her big brown titties. I tongued her right nipple until it hardened, then her left, massaging each one equally.

"Oh *yesssss,*" she hissed.

As I raised up to pull off my shirt, she wiggled her dress down her flat stomach and scooped it past her midsection and kicked it off the bed. I was coming out of my clothes when she turned over onto her stomach, prone. Her butt cheeks were so round and inviting, when I got my dick out, the tip was glistening with pre-cum already.

She looked back at me and gasped. "Damn, Faheem. Yo dick is *huge,* boy! It's probably bigger than my arm. Let me see—" She started to get up but I stopped her.

"Stay there," I ordered. "Don't touch. Just feel."

I laid on top of her, careful not to put the full weight of my frame on her small body. I let my dick rest between her ass cheeks, a hotdog in the bun—and then I stroked back and forth, the underside of my shaft dragging across her asshole, back and forth. I thrust forward all the way, until my ballsack rested against her taint. Then I slid all the way back, enough to see her asshole instantly pucker in, as if to say *not in here with that big ol' dick*.

She flinched when I kissed her asshole.

"Oh!" she squealed, then laughed.

I worked my hands up under her, jacking her pussy in the air. I took turns tonguing her clit and her asshole. I let the tip of my nose tickle the stretch of flesh between both openings, her sensitive perineum. I gobbled her up.

"Oh my fuckin' God!" she screamed.

Her cum juices drizzled.

"Keep doing that," she moaned.

"What?"

"With your nose. And your tongue."

I pressed my nose so flat against her taint, I was able to lick half of her pussy. She moaned, and then she started to wiggle her booty cheeks, a crude style of twerking but fairly safe for my face.

"Oooooh, yes!" She kept bouncing her ass. "Eat it, Faheem, eat it!"

I changed my grip, now clawing into the top of her ass cheeks to spread them up and apart, as I licked and sucked her ass and pussy. She let out a wheezing sound, like she was trying to surrender. Then she placed the soles of her feet against my abs, perhaps to push me back or keep my tongue at bay.

But I wasn't budging.

"*Yeessss!*" she climaxed. "Oh God ..." She pulled her knees in suddenly, then crawled away from me, over to her nightstand. She pulled her laptop onto the bed. "Timeout," she breathed, as she lifted the monitor up. "I just got an idea for Assad."

I chuckled. "You're about to start writing?"

"Yes. I'm forgetful. If I don't write it down right now, the idea will be lost forever. I hate when I forget a good idea."

With my johnson rock hard and dry, I crawled over to her and had a seat next to her. She took my meat in her left hand and started stroking it passively, as she used her right to navigate her laptop's touchpad.

She was multi-tasking.

I watched her work. The on-screen arrow clicked a file, then opened up a writing document. I saw the title. It read: *Petty 2, second draft.*

"How many drafts do you write?" I asked.

"As many as it takes," she replied. "I don't stop drafting until I'm satisfied with the story."

She clicked the touchpad and traced downward, scrolling to the middle of the story where there was a gap of white space. Then she stopped fondling my erection and started typing with all ten fingers.

> *Assad Blackwell's tongue had no end. He flicked it within the crack of her ass, titillating her clit and sucking on her asshole as if he was trying to extract evil spirits orally. As he gripped Andrea's ass cheeks tight—causing a sting of tolerable pain—she placed her feet against his stomach, feeling the ripples of his abdomen against her soles. She thought her feet would act as a barrier, allowing her to limit how deep his tongue went. But oh was she wrong. He was amazingly forceful. She loved his manliness. Ever since her husband's murder, she had never let a man have this much control over her body.*

Then Phaedra closed the laptop and set it back on the nightstand.

"Evil spirits orally?" I said, grinning. "That was a mouthful. No pun intended."

Her brow creased. "You think it was too baroque?"

"I wouldn't know. I write a little bit in my spare time, but you're the professional."

"I don't think one bestselling book classifies me as a professional. But thank you. I might go back and change up some of the words later." Then she smiled. "Now where were we?"

I looked down at my woody.

She wasted no more time—she lowered her head and, with no hands, she taste-tested the head of my dick. *"Mmmm,"* she moaned pleasantly. She rolled her head in circles, giving my sensitive tip a cyclone effect. I bared my teeth as if it hurt, but it was just entirely too erotic.

Then she finally grabbed my meat, spit on it and sucked me nastily. "This is so fuckin' good, Faheem," she said, pausing to rub her clit. "Nice and fat. It makes my jaws work overtime. I'm gonna keep you," she said hoarsely.

Keep me? I wondered.

But the thought left my mind as my dick hit the back of her throat. Her head was *so good.* She started smacking my dick against her long tongue. Then I started to feel dizzy, as if I was entering some kind of dark abyss.

"Fuck me, Faheem," she said. "I need that big monster in me *now.*"

Feeling sluggish, I laid her on her back and guided my dick between her pussy lips. The deeper I got, the louder she moaned. Once I worked up a good steady stroke, I lifted her by the backs of her thighs and pushed her knees to her chest.

I fucked her hard, as she rubbed her clit in circles ferociously.

"Oooooh! I'm cumming!" she screamed.

"I think I am too, Phae."

I held out as long as I could, then I slid out of her and ejaculated on her stomach. Then we both climbed out of bed. I started to get dressed while she opened her laptop again.

I was tying my shoes when I asked her, "Another idea hit you?"

She didn't answer. She was too into her work.

I stood up. "Are you gonna show me out?"

After a short moment, she realized I had asked her a question. "Excuse me?"

"I said, 'Are you gonna walk me to the door?"

"Uh ..." She looked at the words on her screen, then back at me. "You know how to get out, don't you? I rarely ever get a rush of ideas like this. I don't wanna lose my thought."

"Sure. I'll call you later. Tomorrow maybe."

"Sounds good." She turned to her monitor and started typing again. "Thank you, Faheem. I had fun."

"Me too."

I gave her a little wave goodbye that she didn't see, then I turned and walked out of her room. An awkward feeling of inadequacy brewed in my gut as I descended the staircase.

What just happened? Is the movie prospect still on the table? Or did I get used for sex and thrown to the side like Rayshawn?

Then a more positive thought came to mind: *She said she was gonna "keep you," so I must've did something right. I put it down. No reason to doubt myself. I'm the man.*

At the bottom of the staircase, I heard a door open and looked down the hallway. I saw Phaedra's heavyset sister coming out of the basement. Our eyes met, and she smiled at me. But there was an air of connivance in her smile; it made me feel like she had been watching me have sex with her sister. But how could that be? Especially if she was just now reaching the first floor.

"Bye, Faheem," she said flirtatiously.

"See ya," I said back.

Chapter 14: Rayshawn Meeks

I was kneeling down on my closet floor, looking through piles of clothes and opening up plastic totes, rummaging through the junk inside.

Behind me, my girlfriend Natasha said, "What are you looking for?"

I stood up with an angry grunt, then checked the uppermost closet shelf. "A book," I said curtly.

"What book?"

"A novel."

"*Petty?*" she asked.

I spun around, facing her.

Natasha was sitting on my bed with her legs crossed. She was a beautiful dark-skinned woman with long jet-black hair and a gold nose ring. She was wearing purple scrubs that hid her curvy body. On her feet were floral-patterned clogs. She was a nurse at Regency South Atlanta off Cleveland Avenue.

"How'd you know what book I was looking for?" I asked her, with a hint of guilt.

She said, "It's damn near the only book you own."

"Where is it?"

"It's in my desk at work."

My brow creased. "What the fuck is it doing there?"

"I took it to work to read it. You don't read."

"I need that book, Natasha."

"Okay," she said bluntly. "When I go to work tonight I'll bring it home with me. I'm almost done with it anyway. It's good. I would've been done reading it, but I was stretching it out because I don't want it to end."

I sighed. I needed that book right now. Regency South Atlanta would take at least an hour to get to at this time of day. My best bet was to get a new one at the bookstore. There was one maybe ten minutes away from here.

"Why do you wanna read it all of a sudden?" Natasha asked me, skeptical.

"Because me and Faheem are trying to talk the author into turning her book into a movie."

"Oh." She smiled. "You had me worried for a minute. I thought you might've been fuckin' that bitch. I seen her autograph on the first page and thought, 'When did this nigga get her to sign this?' Then I Googled her and saw she had a recent book signing at the Atlanta-Fulton Public Library. Is that where you got it signed?"

"Yes."

"Just checking."

"Grow up. You always thinkin' I'm cheating on you, girl."

"Because you've done it in the past, Rayshawn."

"Prove it."

"The pictures I found in yo phone wasn't proof enough?"

"I told you I got hacked."

She pursed her lips. "Somebody hacked naked pictures *into* yo phone?"

"Yes! They do that type of shit every day!"

Rolling her eyes, she said, "I'm not going down that road again with you. Not right now." Then she added, "And wouldn't no bigtime author like her want yo out-of-shape ass anyway." She laughed.

I shot her a look and she laughed harder. But I really didn't think that was funny. She wouldn't have either if she knew I had already boned said bigtime author.

A half hour ago, I sent Phaedra a text telling her that she had me pegged wrong. I wasn't a bad guy. I stretched the truth sometimes, but in my profession you had to mislead and deceive people in order to get everybody to work together as a cohesive whole. It was hard for me to turn that deception on and off; it was on by default when I was pursuing her. She texted me back saying: *So your lies are turned*

off now? I texted back: *Yes!!!* with three exclamation points because I was happy that she responded back to me as quickly as she did. And then she asked me if I had read her book yet ... and that was when I fucked up.

I told her yes I had read it. Then she texted me a question pertaining to her book, a question about the main character's career before she got married. I quickly logged out of the texting app by thumbing my phone's home screen button, then I brought up the internet with another quick thumb tap. I typed in "Andrea" and "Petty" in the search box. After I hit the magnifying glass icon, a wealth of unrelated information popped up that I didn't have time to sift through. So I refined my search. I typed in "Andrea main character" and "Petty by Phaedra Hodges." This time it was a match—webpage after webpage of Phaedra's bestselling book, pictures of her with fans on social media, and endless quotes from her novel.

But after fifteen minutes of clicking on links, I still couldn't find what Andrea's profession was before she got married. By chance, I saw a snippet of Phaedra's author bio, where it stated she was a real estate agent before she was a writer. Knowing that the main character Andrea was based on Phaedra's real life, I assumed she used her real life career in her book. I texted her back: *real estate agent*, and she put back: *WRONG* in all caps. I quickly sent her: *Sorry, that text wasn't for you.* And just as prompt, she texted: *LOL! Well what was Andrea's career then?*

I hadn't texted her back yet. I started searching for her autographed hardback book, deciding to force myself to read it to avoid getting another wrong answer. I really wanted to fuck Phaedra again. At least one more time.

"Did I hurt your feelings?" Natasha teased as I crossed the room.

"Nope, I know my strengths," I said, grabbing my car keys off the dresser. "And it's not in fitness. It's in my pants."

She glowered at me. "And it better stay in your pants. Negro, where are you going?"

"To the bookstore."

"Now? You're gonna buy that girl's book again? You can't chill with me until it's time for me to go to work, then you can leave too?"

"Nah, baby, I gotta go now. Opportunity comes to those who wait, but only the leftovers of those who hustle."

"I'm the one who told you that quote," she barked as I started heading out of the room. "Hey, come back! You can just download the e-book on your phone!"

I turned. "The what?"

"The e-book. Here, give me your cell phone. I'll download a free book app for you and then you can download her book. I'll show you how to do it. Give me your phone."

I wasn't very skilled in the realm of apps and e-books. I had trouble with the apps I already owned and I didn't have time to learn a new one. Plus, if I gave her my phone I probably wouldn't have gotten it back. And then I'd have to explain all of my new inappropriate sex texts and nude screenshots. The last time she went through my phone she didn't speak to me for a week.

"Nah, Natasha, I need the real book. If I look at my phone screen for too long, it hurts my eyes."

"Since when?" she questioned, but I was already making my exit. "Rayshawn! Since when?!"

***

At the bookstore, I didn't have to search long for Phaedra's work. She had her own little New York Times Bestseller table of novels and bookmarks right up front.

I grabbed a hardback copy.

"Good choice," said the female teller, as she placed my book in a bag. "Did you know that Phaedra Hodges is a local author?"

"Yes, I heard." Then I started to walk off. But I paused, turned back. "Have you read this book yet?"

"Oh yeah. Fascinating story about domestic violence and perseverance. I read it twice."

"What was the main character's profession before she got married?"

"Real estate agent," she said.

"No, not the real author's occupation. The character based on her. Andrea."

"Real estate agent," she repeated adamantly. "Phaedra made Andrea have the same profession as her. The whole book was taken from her own life, almost verbatim. Except name changes. That's what made the book so good."

Son of a bitch, I thought.

Once I got back home, I took my jacket off and threw it over the back of the couch. Then I plopped down on the couch cushions and stared at the cover of the book.

"*Petty,*" I said aloud, reading the title. "Yeah, you are petty, Ms. Phaedra Hodges."

Faheem told me he slept with her last week. He said he didn't plan to. He said he just wanted to keep it professional, talk about movie rights over dinner and leave her with a positive impression of his competence in the movie business. But then she invited him to her room—and it went down. I told him that was the same way it happened to me. When I asked him if he was able to follow up with her, he told me no. He hadn't heard from her since they had sex. We both were in agreement now: "We got used for sex."

In his opinion, we needed to just leave Phaedra alone and let her contact us whenever she was ready to do business.

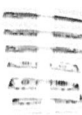

He made it a point to tell me *twice* to stay away from her because she didn't trust me.

But Faheem failed to realize sometimes how good I was at changing people's minds. And how I hated to sit around and wait for good things to fall in my lap.

All I needed to do was get Phaedra to trust me again.

So I opened up her book and started reading ...

Chapter 15: Faheem Mathis

Bang! Bang! Bang!

I reared up in my bed, looking around my room in a panic. I quickly grabbed my phone; my lock screen flashed 2:57 a.m. There was no reason for someone to be downstairs beating on my front door.

Bang! Bang! Bang!

I climbed out of bed and threw on my silk robe. Walking to my dresser, I squatted down and reached underneath it. I pulled out a polymer-framed Glock 17. It was covered in dust.

As I walked down my steps to the first floor with the gun at my side, I had no fear of the unwanted guest. I was just irritated that I was losing precious sleep. Each step down was a slow, heavy footfall.

Finally, I looked through the peephole. It was Rayshawn.

Figures, I thought.

I opened the door.

"Faheem!" he shouted, even though we were face to face. "I read the book! I read Phaedra's book!"

He was holding the novel up, waving it in my face as if it were the Holy Bible. I pushed him back and slammed my door, but he shoved it back open before I had a chance to lock it.

"Faheem, you're gonna wanna hear what I have to say about this book," he stated vehemently, as he marched in my house and started pacing back and forth in long strides.

"What's wrong with you?" I asked dryly.

"This book is a confession!"

"A what?"

"Phaedra really did kill her husband and his mistress!"

I stared at him in confusion, then I walked over to my staircase. I barely got one foot on the first step before he grabbed my arm.

"Listen to me!" he pleaded.

"No, Rayshawn. You're just excited because this is the first good book you've read in a while. Probably ever."

"That's not it. I know what I'm talking about. Phaedra cleverly hid the truth in this book. She's a killer. And she had an accomplice."

I said, "Join her fan club, Rayshawn."

"Man, I'm serious!"

"Me too! Phaedra has a fan club online where readers debate back and forth about why she's either guilty or not guilty. People fact-check the real investigation of her husband and his mistress's disappearance and compare it to her book. A lot of people have claimed that they've 'figured it out.'" I threw up quotation fingers. "But the truth is: if she did it, she would be in jail."

"Faheem, just hear me out. Listen to what I have to say."

Sighing, I sat down on the steps and placed my dusty gun on my lap. "You have two minutes. We're both supposed to be at the studio in four hours. I don't know about you, but I'm not well-rested yet."

"It won't take that long," he said, and then he clumsily opened up the book to a page where he had affixed a yellow sticky note. He pointed to a paragraph. "This is the scene where the mistress, Tracy Pritchard, is introduced for the first time. Phaedra describes her as"—he reads the passage with his finger—"*a woman with meat on her bones.* After she and Shamar have sex, she shows him to the door and says, *'Don't let the door hit ya where the Good Lord split ya.'* That right there sent up a red flag for me. You wanna know how?"

I didn't. But he was waiting on me to respond. "How, Rayshawn?" I said to speed things up.

"That's the same thing her sister Patricia said to me after I left her house. *Don't let the door hit ya where the Good Lord split ya.* This is *after* I heard somebody scream for help in their basement."

He looked at me as if I was supposed to realize something. But I didn't get his point.

"Patricia is the mistress!" Rayshawn announced. "Even the names sound alike—Patricia West, Tracy Pritchard; Tracy Pritchard, Patricia West. I think Patricia helped Phaedra kill the husband. That's why Phaedra had an airtight alibi."

"So who do you think was in the basement screaming? They're killing more people?"

"Maybe her husband had more mistresses and she's killing them all."

"First you said Phaedra was the killer. Now you're saying Patricia is. Which one is it?"

"I don't know for sure who pulled the trigger or how it went down. I haven't read the real investigation. But I know both of 'em are guilty of murder in one way or another."

I shook my head, feeling sorry for him. "Rayshawn, writers do that all the time. They take attributes and idiosyncrasies—even names—from people they know in real life and apply them to their characters. Phaedra took some features from her sister, so what? That makes them guilty? No, shawty. That's what makes the characters seem real."

"I knew you'd doubt me. I doubted myself. So I kept reading. And I found this." He flipped through some more pages in the novel, where there was another sticky note bookmarked. He held the pages open to me, displaying both odd and even page. He had a paragraph highlighted on the odd page that I guessed I was supposed to read aloud.

I shook my head again. "Just tell me your theory, please."

"In this scene, the lead detective still hasn't found the bodies of the main mistress and the husband, and the trail is running thin. So he goes to the dead mistress's mother's house and questions her again."

I chimed in. "Mrs. Doherty shows Detective Huey Albitron a picture of Shamar and her daughter Robin Doherty together," I said impatiently. "The detective sees a ring on Robin's ring finger. It turns out that Shamar got engaged to Robin and was planning to divorce Andrea. Rayshawn, I've read the story already, remember?"

He smiles big, way too excited. "Yes! So you know that Mrs. Doherty told the detective that her daughter's ring had the initials S and R?"

"Yes," I agreed. "And at the end of the book, the other mistress that killed them both kept the ring as a keepsake."

He pointed at me fast. "*Exactly!* And guess what I found at Phaedra's house under her couch? A ring with the initials I and D! In the book it was S and R for Shamar and Robin. But in real life it's I and D for Isaiah and Delana!"

At that, I got up and started up my steps.

"You don't believe me?" he asked.

"No," I said, still lumbering upward. "But I believe you just wasted my time. Phaedra is a nympho, not a killer."

"The ring is real! I saw it with my own eyes!"

Once I got to the second floor, I turned and looked down at him. "Do you really expect me to believe that Phaedra and Patricia killed those people and they keep a dead girl's ring under the couch in the living room? Give me a fucking break?"

"Killers keep trophies of their kills all the time," he said in the same mocking tone I had used when explaining away his theory that Tracy Pritchard was based off Patricia.

"Goodnight, Rayshawn. Or good morning. No, better yet—*goodbye.*"

"I bet the ring has DNA evidence on it."

"Tell me this, Rayshawn: Why do you even care? Wait, I'll answer that. It's because she doesn't wanna give you no more pussy and your ego is hurt and now you're on this stupid crusade to prove to me she's guilty of murder. You know what, Rayshawn ... ? You should write a book called *Mr. Petty.*"

"I admit, I am a little salty that she kicked us to the curb."

"You're salty that she kicked *you* to the curb," I corrected him. "You don't give a shit that she curbed me too."

I saw a glimmer of a smile appear on his face, then it disappeared. "It's about more than that, Faheem. We could be saving lives. Who knows how many women they have in that basement. It's a big fuckin' house! Imagine how big that basement is and what they're capable of doing down there. We already know how twisted Phaedra is." He held up the book and pointed to it, as if the fictional murder/mystery proved Phaedra had a criminal mind.

I turned away, walked in my room and slammed the door.

Chapter 16: Rayshawn Meeks

At work, I tried to convince Faheem again that Phaedra's book was truth disguised as fiction. "Phaedra and her sister Patricia are murderers!" I said emphatically. I had read the book again and found more clues. He didn't want to hear it.

"Have you even been to sleep?" he asked me with irritation, as he shifted in his director's chair.

"No. I can't sleep. I tried."

"Go home, Rayshawn."

"I'm fine. I'm here. I'll shut up about Phaedra, okay?"

He seemed skeptical. "The stunt double we had scheduled for the day canceled on us," he informed me. "I need you to find another one that can show up in the next three hours. Has to be a brown-skinned woman. Or a brown-skinned male stunt double with feminine features."

"No problem. I'm on it."

But by the time I sat down at a computer with accessible Wi-Fi, I had forgotten what Faheem asked me to do.

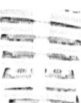

Instead, I was typing "missing persons in Atlanta" in the search box. I was amazed by how many African-American women in Atlanta had disappeared in the last year alone. *Why haven't I seen none of this on the news?* I thought with concern.

Then I came across an article about a missing dancer from Decatur. Her real name was Erikka Brown; her stripper name was simply Geechee. In her mugshot, a big flower tattoo blossomed up her fair-skinned neck in pink and yellow petals. She was one of the few missing Atlanta girls with a video clip on the WSB-TV Channel 2 website because—get this: *She was rumored to be romantically involved with the missing real estate mogul Isaiah Hodges.*

"This can't be a coincidence," I said out loud. "Phaedra is killing—and probably torturing—all of her husband's side chicks ..."

I bolted across the studio in the middle of a live scene and tugged on Faheem's arm. I told him what I had discovered and he hollered:

"Get your ass off of me! Go home, Rayshawn. Go sleep that shit off!"

Knowing he wouldn't believe me without proof, I left. But I didn't go home ...

RICH & PETTY

***

This was my first time driving through Tuxedo Park in the daytime. The entire neighborhood was so prestigious. Every home had a huge lot nestled into the woods. As Phaedra's mansion appeared, I noticed for the first time that she had a terraced garden that wrapped around the east side of her home. That was the side I parked on, the east side—closer to her neighbor's house so I'd look like her neighbor's guest.

I watched the mansion closely. Without taking my eyes off of it, I plucked my cup of black coffee from this rented Bentley's center console and took a long, slow sip. The coffee seemed like it wasn't helping. My eyelids were growing heavier by the second.

From checking Phaedra's tour schedule, I knew she wasn't home right now. She was in Toronto, and tomorrow she would be in Chicago. But Patricia was home. I assumed this because the Porsche Panamera was parked in the driveway.

I slowly closed my eyes, resting them. Then I opened them again, rolling my neck to keep myself awake. But a moment later my eyes fell shut again ...

... And by the time they opened back up, it was night time. Phaedra's mansion was pitch black. And the Porsche Panamera was gone!

Suddenly alert, I opened the door and stepped out of the Bentley. I didn't bother to lock it because the horn would honk. Stealthily, I crept up Phaedra's lawn, sticking close to the row of privacy hedges that acted as a fence between her and the neighbor's property. I climbed up close to the side of the mansion through the muddy garden and started walking toward the back yard.

It was darkest close to the house. I felt hidden. I felt safe.

Then: *Ring! Ring! Ring!*

My phone was going off. I quickly tore it out of pocket and answered it.

"Hello?"

"Where are you?" Natasha asked me.

"I'm at work. Look, I can't talk right now."

"Okay. I was just calling to let you know I finished Phaedra's book. It was so damn good. You better be careful working with that bitch. I think she's the real killer."

"Me too."

"You read the book already?" she asked, surprised.

"Yes."

"That fast? Damn, I'm proud of you. I didn't think you'd make it all the way to the end, let alone beat me reading it."

"Natasha, can I call you back?"

"Sure. I just wanted to let you know you can have your book back, even though you already read it. Oh, and there's a sex scene in there ... you know, the one between Shamar and Robin?"

"Yeah."

"That joint was hot! Phaedra has a vivid imagination. Maybe you and me can reenact that scene when I get home."

The thought of roleplaying one of Phaedra's fictional sex scenes with Natasha might've turned me on before, but right now the thought made my skin crawl. I told Natasha I'd talk to her later, then I powered my phone completely off.

"Now how am I gon' get in this bitch?" I said to myself, as I stood on the back patio, staring at the back doors. I tried the knobs in vain. Then I stepped into the grass of the back-yard lawn, far enough back to take in the mansion's entire rear presentation.

I saw a possible way in. Second floor terrace. There was a door.

Deciding to give it a try, I dragged the patio table close to the house. Then I climbed on top of it, pausing a moment to keep my balance because the table's legs were wobbly. From here, I was able to grab onto the lower rail of the second level terrace. Then I brought one foot up, hook-ing it in between two posts; this gave me enough leverage to heave myself upward. Once I got ahold of the top rail, I was able to pull myself up and over it.

"Maybe I'm not so out of shape after all," I said to myself once I was standing on the terrace. I had my hands on my hips, breathing hard as if I had just run track.

Then I tried the terrace door.

It was open.

And it led me into Phaedra's master bedroom.

Chapter 17: Phaedra Hodges

I would've never known I had so many Canadian fans. My publicist, Sarah Maturo, was right—I needed to get out of Atlanta more often.

After one more selfie with a young girl with glittering metal braces, Sarah took my hand and pulled me into the rear seats of a black GMC Yukon Denali. A waving crowd of young and old readers sent me off and I waved back like a happy little kid.

I feel like royalty!

"You ready for Chicago?" Sarah asked me, as our chauffeur drove us down a street called Yonge.

"Yes!" I said cheerfully.

"Good. We have about thirty or forty minutes before we get to the airport. I need you to drop a picture or two on social media and start interacting with your fans."

I frowned. "That's Patricia's job."

"Patricia's not here. And you need to be more hands-on anyway. I like it when you post and interact. When Patricia does it, she comes off as ..."

"Bitchy?" I offered.

"I was gonna say brusque, but yes—Patricia is too mean-spirited sometimes. She reacts more to the negative comments than she does the positive ones. She spends too much time trying to convince the online trolls that you're not a murderer."

"Okay," I said, pulling out my phone. "I'll log in."

"Thank you."

I planned on doing exactly as my publicist had instructed, but first I had to check my surveillance app. It was a habit. Two or three times a day when I was away from home—especially out of the country—I had to check my interior surveillance cameras to see what was going on inside my house, making sure Phaedra was handling her duties appropriately. I imagined this was what my husband did after he installed the cameras—he'd sit with one of his side chicks in some faraway hotel and check this app every so often. Spying on me. Making sure I wasn't cheating—like him.

Once the surveillance app appeared on my screen, I tapped the first monitor's thumbnail and it expanded full screen. It was live footage of the darkness of my front entryway, but the night vision feature brightened my home with shades of fluorescent green, allowing me to see details otherwise naked to the human eye. From here, I swiped my thumb and the kitchen appeared. I saw nothing. Another swipe—living room, nothing out of the ordinary.

Then I swiped again. This time my master bedroom appeared—and I saw a man lurking through it with a fluorescent green skin tone!

"Oh my God!" I screamed.

"What is it?!" Sarah asked, just as freaked out as me.

"Somebody's in my home!"

She looked at my phone screen. Her eyes exploded. "Is that live?!"

"Yes!"

"You need to call the police, Phaedra. No, I'll do it. I can get a line directly to Atlanta PD."

I grabbed her wrist. "No. Don't call the police."

"Why?"

I hesitated. "Because ... it might not be a burglar. It might be one of Patricia's friends."

"Phaedra, that's clearly somebody wandering through your house in the dark. We need to let the police sort it out."

"Let me call Patricia first."

"Okay. Hurry. If she doesn't answer, I'm calling the police."

I dialed Patricia. She answered on the second ring.

"Hey, girl," she said.

"Patricia, where are you?!"

"I'm at the grocery store. Why do you sound so—?"

"Get home now!"

"Why? I locked the basement door. I checked it twice before I left."

"Somebody is in my bedroom!"

She gasped. "Is it the—?"

I cut her off. "No, somebody is breaking *in*, not out. Get home now!"

She hung up without another word.

Beside me, Sarah had her thumb hovering over her phone's keypad. "Can I call now?" she asked me impatiently.

"No," I said. "Patricia is handling it."

"Handling it how?"

"It has to be somebody we know."

"What if it's not?"

"Sarah, just drop it. She's taking care of it."

I looked at the surveillance on my phone and saw the intruder leaving my master bedroom. Swiping to a new monitor, I now saw him walking down my staircase. My heartrate spiked.

"Cancel Chicago," I said to Sarah.

"What?" she asked.

"I said cancel Chicago!" I shouted. "I need to get back to Atlanta right now!"

Chapter 18: Rayshawn Meeks

As I headed downstairs, my hand slid along the wooden rail. I wasn't worried about fingerprints because they were already embedded from my last visit. I was more worried about missing a step—I could barely see anything in this darkness. If I tumbled down and broke a bone, there was no explaining what I was doing here. I'd be hauled off to jail.

Once I reached the first floor, I hooked the corner and headed down the hallway past the kitchen. There were splashes of moonlight on the floor and walls here and there that helped light my path, but I still felt half blind.

My first mission was to find out who or what was in the basement. The closer I got to the basement door though, the more my adrenaline picked up.

I was nervous and starting to perspire. It was so quiet in here I could hear a loud ringing in my ears. Then my gut started to speak to me: *This is a bad idea, Rayshawn.*

Ignoring my better sense—as I had done most of my life—I approached the basement door and placed my hand on the knob. It was cold to the touch. I turned it; sure enough it was locked.

With a knuckle, I knocked on the center of the door. *Tap. Tap. Tap.* The knock sounded dull, as if there was some kind of reinforcement or soundproofing behind the door. Rested an ear against it, I listened for the faintest of sounds.

Skkkrttt!

I instantly jerked my head around. I knew the sound of Porsche tires anywhere. And I was staring at a set of headlights washing over the front of the house, illuminating half of the interior and casting scary shadows everywhere.

"Oh shit! Patricia's back!"

I ran back to the staircase, planning to escape the same way I came in. But then I remembered what I came here for—the ring!

A car door slammed hard outside. Then I saw a large silhouette through the stained glass of the front door.

I didn't have time to grab the ring!

Racing up the steps, I heard Patricia fumbling with the front door lock. I propelled myself across the hall and into the master bedroom just as the front door came bursting open, banging against the back wall.

"I know you're in here!" she hollered.

I pressed my back against the bedroom wall, directly adjacent to the bedroom door. I was trying not to breathe so loud. *How did she know somebody had broken in? Silent alarm?*

Discreetly, I peered around the doorframe in slow motion, a millimeter at a time, just enough to peek with one eye. Patricia was standing in the entryway with a phone to her ear.

In her other hand was a firearm.

"Where is he?" she barked into the phone. "Upstairs? Which room?"

Who was she talking to? I wondered. *And how do they know where—?*

The camera! I realized.

I bolted across the room and threw the door open that put me back outside onto the rear terrace. Acting off adrenaline, I sprinted for the edge.

And I jumped over the railing.

I fell fast.

Left foot hit the dirt first.

Crack!

"Aaarggh! Shit!" I cried out, holding my left ankle, writhing on the ground in pain. But I quickly pulled myself to my feet and hobbled toward the side of the house.

Bang! Bang!

I heard the shots and felt the bullets zip past my head. I dove forward into a roll, and to the best of my ability I

pushed off my lower back and butt and came back up to my feet semi-gracefully. I was now up against the side of the house, out of Patricia's line of fire.

My ankle was screaming!

I hobbled along though, sticking close to the mansion's rusticated siding that looked like stone. I slid through the garden, down against the privacy hedges and made a fast break—a crippled fast break—for my Bentley.

"Oh fuck oh fuck shit!" I cursed in a panic once I got my hands on my driver's side door handle.

I thrust the door open, climbed in and cranked the engine, slamming my door at the same time.

Then I sped off.

Chapter 19: Rayshawn Meeks

"How's your leg?" Faheem asked me.

"You mean my ankle?" I replied.

I looked down at my feet, which were resting in the passenger seat footwell of Faheem's Range Rover. My fractured left foot was Velcroed into a foot brace with metal-reinforced uprights and a foam liner. The foot was supposed to be elevated, but I got tired of sitting around the studio so I joined Faheem on a lunch run.

We were at a standstill behind a minivan, in the drive-thru of a Chick-fil-A off Peachtree Street.

"How the hell did you slam your foot in the car door?" He looked over at me as if I was the stupidest person in the world.

"Moving too fast," I said.

"I know that shit had to hurt too. Those Bentley doors are heavy as fuck."

"Still hurts, muthafucka."

He chuckled. "Who the hell were you running from to be moving that fast?"

"Nobody," I lied.

"Nah, shawty, you was running from somebody. You probably got caught up at some bitch's house. Her nigga came home and you started running for your life. That's karma, Rayshawn. You need to leave them hoes alone. You got a good girl in Natasha. She's pretty. She's smart. She's a nurse, so she don't lean on you for financial support. Watch what I tell you. Two or three years from now you gon' regret the way you're treating her. She's gon' be the one that got away."

I thought about telling Faheem what really happened to my foot. But I already had a good idea what his response would be. He'd scream at me and tell me that I had crossed the line. In truth, I felt that I had.

Since the break-in, three days had passed. No police had come knocking on my door and I hadn't gotten an angry phone call or inquiring text from Phaedra.

I was in the clear. And I had no more desire to play detective ever again.

Our vehicle inched forward. We were still two cars back from receiving our food.

Faheem's phone rang. He looked at the caller ID and his face lit up. "It's Phaedra!" he exclaimed.

My heart stopped. "Who?"

He answered the phone. "Hello?"

Faheem started off doing a lot of listening. He'd utter an "Uh-huh" or a "Yeah, sure," but nothing that tipped me off to what they were talking about. I assumed it wasn't about breaking and entering because he winked at me excitedly.

I was still nervous as fuck though. And my ankle had suddenly started throbbing again.

Faheem glanced over at me. "Yeah, he's right here next to me," he said into the phone.

My eyes went wide.

"Yeah. Uh-huh. I'll let him know. A'ight, you take care. Bye." He hung up his phone. "Yes!"

"What?" I asked.

"Phaedra says she's interested in working with us. She wants us to come over tomorrow evening to negotiate royalties."

"Why all of a sudden?"

"She said she looked me up and saw some of my work. She watched *Real Girls* online and thought it was brilliant. She loved the cinematography." He rubbed his hands together greedily. "Yes, Lord! She saw your name in the credits too and she wants to give you another shot at honesty. Don't fuck this up again, Rayshawn. You really read the book, right?"

"Yeah, I read it. But I'm not too sure about messing with her again. This could be some kind of a trap."

"A trap? Did you say a trap? Please don't tell me you're still on that murder stuff."

"Something doesn't feel right about this."

"The only thing that doesn't feel right is your foot," he joked. "I think you got that brace on too tight. If Phaedra Hodges wants me to meet up with her again to talk business, then I'm all for it. If you don't wanna go, then that's on you. I'll tell her you broke your foot."

It went without saying—there was no talking Faheem out of this. His mind was set. And one thing I knew I couldn't let him do was go over Phaedra's house alone. If those girls were planning to try something funny, then we stood a better chance of coming out of there alive if we stuck together.

"I'm going," I said finally.

"I knew you was," he said.

Chapter 20: Rayshawn Meeks

Faheem opened the passenger side door for me, as if he were my valet.

"I can get out on my own," I said, irritated. "I got a fractured foot. I'm not a paraplegic."

"Hey—I'm just trying to help," he snapped back. "Chill out. Don't be going in there with no attitude."

"I'm just saying," I said.

I swung my right foot out, then my oversized foot brace. As I grabbed the door handle to hoist myself up to my feet, Faheem jerked the door, feigning slamming it, and I flinched so hard I fell back into my seat.

He burst into laughter. "You pussy," he cracked.

"Fuck you," I growled.

He offered to help me up to the door but I declined. I hobbled beside him instead. A thought occurred to me: *If something does go awry, I might be more of a hindrance to Faheem than help. Maybe I should have stayed at home after all.*

He knocked on the door and Phaedra pulled it open almost immediately.

"Hi, guys," she said, smiling. "Come on in."

Too late to change my mind now, I thought.

As we entered, I took a subtle glance at Phaedra's jaw-dropping dress. It was a close cut all-white number with a split hem. Her hair was big and curly and tinged with a raspberry hue. A thin gold and diamond bracelet sparkled on her left wrist, and from my experience with jewelry I was sure she forked over at least ten bands for it.

"Rayshawn, what happened to your foot?" she asked me with a pained face.

"Car door," I said.

"Do you want me to get a wheelchair for you? We have one."

"Yall keep a wheelchair here?" I asked.

"Yes."

Faheem butted in. "Oh no, don't offer to help him. He's sensitive about being cripple."

I ignored him and addressed Phaedra: "Thanks, but I'll be okay walking. It hurts a little but I'm trying to force my way through it."

"O-kay," she said, drawing out each syllable as if I was missing out on a good deal. "This way, guys. Patricia already set the table."

"Can't wait," Faheem said. "If it's anything like her last meal, I know it's gon' be good."

We walked down the hall, Phaedra taking the lead. I kept pace, despite wanting to stop and sit down and rest my foot. When we finally did take our seats at the dining room table, Patricia walked in carrying a bowl of red Jell-O. She set it on the table along with the rest of the food—cheesy taco lasagna, ham and cheese tortellini, Asian noodle salad, and chicken and broccoli.

Me and Patricia's eyes met for a brief moment, then she looked away.

Faheem kicked off the first question: "So what kind of contract do you and your publisher have as far as movie rights?"

"Fifty-fifty," Phaedra replied.

"Not bad."

"I have a good agent."

"Will your agent get a cut of your movie profits?"

"Fifteen percent. But that's not a problem. She deserves it. Her name is Sarah Maturo. She's my agent, my publicist, my etiquette coach, my bodyguard, and my personal assistant. I wouldn't be where I'm at today without her."

They continued to talk business, and I stayed out of it for the most part. Strangely, whenever I looked across the table at Patricia, she'd cut her eyes somewhere else,

pretending she hadn't been staring at me. *Does she know it was me that broke in?* I wondered. *If she knows, why hasn't she said anything?*

Rotating my fork, I rolled strings of Asian noodles up and stuffed them in my mouth. It tasted good. Damn good. Hints of brown sugar and hot pepper sauce tickled my palate.

"Do *you* have any questions for me?" Phaedra asked me, smiling. She caught me off guard. "All quiet over there. Acting like a guilty defendant on trial."

I finished chewing my food, wiped my mouth as I shook my head no. "I'm just here for support. I'll leave the questions to him." I nodded at Faheem.

"Well I have some questions for you," she said.

"Go ahead," I said.

"It's a question I already asked you. But first: You read my book, right? No lies. We're starting from scratch, okay?"

"No lies," I agreed. "I read it. Front to back."

"Good. So what was Andrea Howard's career before she married Shamar Howard?"

"Mmm," Faheem moaned excitedly. He threw his hand in the air, waiting to be called on.

Amused, Phaedra shook her head no and pointed at me. "He has to answer it. No phone-a-friend."

"Real estate agent," I stated.

"I told you that was wrong in a text and you texted me back that you made a mistake. You said you texted the wrong person."

"I don't know what I was thinking at that time. But real estate agent is the answer."

"Hmm. Good job. Next question: What is the lead detective's first and last name?"

"Huey Albitron."

"What is Andrea's male interest's name?"

"Assad Blackwell."

Her eyebrows shot up in surprise. My answers were spontaneous. She was impressed. "Okay, okay, Mr. Meeks. Last question: What did Tracy Pritchard use to kill Robin Doherty?"

I glanced at Patricia before answering. "She used a nail file," I said. "She slammed it right into Robin's left eye. And as her victim floundered around on the ground like a fish out of water—your exact words, Phaedra, right?—she jumped on top of her and put her in a stranglehold. You never exactly told the reader which method actually killed Robin; the stabbing in the eye or the strangulation. I guess it doesn't matter. She's dead."

There was a brief moment of silence, as my summary hung in the air.

Then Phaedra looked at Faheem accusatorially. "Did you prep him with the answers before yall came over here?"

"No, ma'am," said Faheem. "He really read the book. He really got a kick out of it too. He came knocking on my door in the middle of night talking about he really thinks you and Patricia killed your husband and his mistress."

I kicked Faheem under the table.

"No, don't kick me. Tell 'em what you think," he carried on. "Tell 'em how you claim you found some kind of mystery ring under the couch in the living room."

Patricia dropped her fork in her plate with a loud clank.

But Phaedra kept her composure. She asked me coolly, "You think I killed my husband and his mistress?"

"Uh ... um ..." I couldn't find the words to defend myself. And my ankle started to throb again. "No ... I ..."

Slowly, Phaedra placed her hand on the butter knife that lay beside her plate. She clutched it in her fist as she rose to her feet, the back of her knees automatically scooting her chair back. Then she walked over to Faheem and stood behind him with the knife. When she put her free hand on his forehead, he voluntarily let her pull his head back as she put the butter knife to his throat.

I was scared shitless. It was just a butter knife, but I knew if enough pressure was applied it could still do some serious damage. I swallowed the lump in my throat.

Phaedra glared at me. "Rayshawn, do you think I could really go through with something like this?"

I was speechless.

"To be honest, I wish I was woman enough to take a man's life," she went on, then flicked her eyes down, staring into Faheem's eyes upside down. The teeth of the butter knife rested against his Adam's apple. "But you wanna know what I'm not scared to take from a man?"

"Uht?" muttered Faheem, trying to say "what."

"His love," she said.

Then she lowered her lips to his, upside down, and kissed him passionately.

"Ewww," said Patricia, wrinkling her nose. "Not at the kitchen table. I just lost my appetite."

Phaedra finished up the kiss with her tongue, then leaned up, allowing Faheem to lean forward. She tossed the butter knife on the table.

"I'll agree to make the movie with you guys under one condition," she said to the both of us, but was looking directly at me. "You guys have to help me with a scene in the sequel. And this particular scene is a ménage a trois."

Chapter 21: Phaedra Hodges

As I walked up the staircase, I looked over my shoulder at my two guests to make sure they were following me. Faheem was taking two steps at a time, right on my ass. Rayshawn, on the other hand, was lagging behind, struggling to get his foot brace up on each new step.

"You need some help?" I asked Rayshawn.

"Nah, I'm right behind yall," he said. "I'm fine."

In the bedroom, I strutted right over to my stereo to set the mood. I cut on an up-tempo classic—En Vogue's "Hold on."

Rayshawn, who had finally made it into the room, cracked a smile.

"Is this song too fast?" I asked the men.

"Good to me," said Faheem.

"That's fine," said Rayshawn. "But can you cut it down some?"

I had wanted to keep the volume high to make sure no unwanted noise travelled into our tryst. But to keep Rayshawn—aka Mr. Skeptical—satisfied, I cut the volume down a couple notches.

"Better?" I asked him.

"Yes," he said.

I started lip syncing the words to the song, as I moved my shoulders in rhythm to the drum pattern, at the same time working my dress off starting from the neck down.

I eyed Rayshawn as I unhooked my bra, singing, *"Don't ... waste your time/ fighting blind/ minded thoughts/ of despair."*

He let out a laugh. And that's what I wanted to hear. I needed to convince him more than Faheem that I wasn't a murderer.

With my breasts out, I rolled my panties down my thighs and stepped out of them. Then I crawled on my bed and laid down on my side provocatively. Lust twinkled in their eyes. As I stared at them both, I trailed the pointed toes of my right foot up my left calf, slow and seductive.

"Who's first?" I asked.

They both took a step forward. Rayshawn was slower, so Faheem held his friend back with a stiff arm. I was surprised when Rayshawn then grabbed the back of Faheem's shirt to pull him back.

Rip.

Faheem looked down at the tear in his shirt. "Shawty, really?"

I interrupted. "The both of you are gonna have your way with me at the same time. I just want one of you to get me ready before the other joins in."

"That's me," said Rayshawn.

"Nah, me," Faheem countered. "You can't handle that like I can. Look at you—you can't even walk."

"I don't need to walk." Faheem held his hands down by his waist and made a pumping action. "I just need to do this. And I do that best."

"I'll decide," I chimed in.

They looked at me, both of them hopeful. I had their undivided attention and obedience.

"Smallest first," I said.

Faheem took a step back. "Be my guest, Rayshawn. She picked you."

I burst into laughter.

Rayshawn didn't move. He placed his hands on his hips.

"Rayshawn, just come on," I begged. "Please, Mr. Meeks."

"Only because the lady asked," Rayshawn said to Faheem, as he started hobbling my way.

He sat down on the edge of the bed and started taking off his shirt. En Vogue was still crooning on the radio. Unstrapping his foot brace, he pulled it off and then removed his other shoe. He crawled near me, covering my body with his—and then he started kissing me on the lips. French kissing. Sucking my tongue.

I opened my legs so his midsection could rest against my pussy. I was starting to warm up.

Then he kissed my neck, working his lips and tongue generously across my collarbone, my breasts, then my tummy. When his lips kissed my center, I hissed.

"*Ssss*. Mmm, Rayshawn. That's it right there."

He put one of my legs over his shoulder and flattened my other leg against the bed with his palm; my pink flower was now wide open. He flicked his tongue over my clitoris fast beyond belief. Flickety-flick-flick. Nonstop clit titillation. Then he lifted his head and squinted his eyes at my folds as if he were dissatisfied.

"What's wrong?" I asked.

"That pearl ain't as ripe as I want it to be yet. Hold on."

He then licked his fingers and pinched the lower half of my pussy lips together, which made my clit pop out further. Then his tongue attacked me again, and I screamed out in ecstasy.

"Yes! Yes!"

White-clearish nectar flowed out of me.

Glancing over at Faheem, I saw he already had his shirt off. And his pants were open, his big dick hanging out in his palm. He was stroking himself, eyeing me intensely, teeth clenched. His meat was bigger than Rayshawn's by at least a full two inches. But Rayshawn was too busy eating my pussy to notice or care.

"C'mon, Faheem," I beckoned him. "I'm ready for you too now, sir."

He came and kneeled down on the bed with his cap in my face. I sucked his whole dick while Rayshawn feasted on my pussy.

"Mmmm," I moaned, as I slurped and slopped up Faheem's fullness. He had his hand behind my head, forcing me to stay glued to his brown shaft.

I was so happy right now. I had written about this very moment over and over for years, erotic stories from my adolescence all the way up to adulthood, but my imagination was proving to be peanuts compared to the feel and smells of two powerful male bodies in the flesh.

Thoughts of Isaiah and Delana beating me with the belt flashed through my mind, but only for a moment.

When I finally got Rayshawn on his back and he pumped his member up into my pussy like a rabbit, I screamed, while Faheem squatted behind me dogging my asshole out. The dual pleasure had my jaw touching my chest like a big yawn frozen in time. I couldn't close my mouth for the life of me.

"Uhhh ... Uhhh ... Uhhh!" I moaned. They each bucked at a different pace, random momentum in and out of me. I was getting teary-eyed from the rich sensations.

Faheem and Rayshawn were amazing individually, but together they were gods.

When the time came, I had no problem laying on my stomach and letting them jack off in my face. Rayshawn nutted first, and I sucked on his cap until Faheem finally splashed me too.

Before I scooted off the bed to wipe their semen off my face, I made sure to look directly in the upper corner of the room and smile.

Chapter 22: Phaedra Hodges

Though I was blindfolded, I knew Assad Blackwell was standing beside the bed in the nude. I could smell his musky scent, and I had a perfect image of his dark chocolate god-like body embedded in my mind. Without warning, he dragged me by the ankles until my bottom was at the edge of the bed, then he maneuvered one of my legs so it rested over the crook of his elbow.

With his other hand, he guided his massive love muscle inside of my moist slit.

"Ooooh!" I squealed. I wanted to remove the blind-fold so bad so I could watch his shaft disappear inside of me. But rules were rules—no peeking.

He started stroking me slowly.

"Good?" he asked, with gruffness in his voice.

"Mmm-hmm," I whimpered like a little girl.

"More?"

"Mmm-hmm."

The second man, the one I was never supposed to see, knelt down on the bed with his knees planted on either side of my shoulders. All I had to do was open my mouth— and he bent his meat down inside my jaws. He carefully let his dickhead nuzzle back and forth along the roof of my mouth, as if this was the only sensation he was looking for. Then he pulled back some, gently finessing his fat mush-room tip between my upper lip and my upper teeth. Then he trailed his cap across my top gums. Another strange form of pleasure for him, I assumed. He did the same gum-stroke to my lower teeth.

I had a nickname for this unknown man already— The Explorer.

Assad was pounding my pussy with glorious effort, and The Explorer had finally let me suck his big penis nor-mally (well, as normal as I could while laying on my back; it was less me and more him—he was fucking my face). Then, as if they had this choreographed, Assad eased out of my womb at the same time The Explorer popped his beef out of my mouth. Someone—I didn't know which one because I was blind—turned me on my side.

Nervously, I let my body slacken as they each moved my limbs into position. One in front of me on his side, draped my arm across him; the other in back on his side, pulled my thigh up to make my forbidden hole more acces-sible. They kept snuggling closer to me, sandwiching me in.

I felt both of their warm breaths on my face, on the back of my neck respectively.

And I loved it!

"You comfortable?" Assad asked me. And from the sound of his voice I knew he was the one that was in front of me.

"I think so. Yes," I said to him, both excited and terrified.

The Explorer said nothing. I flinched when his dickhead touched my asshole, because it was now ice cold with whatever lubricant he'd just applied. He pushed inside of my anus gradually. But gradually or not, his size made entry uncomfortable for me. However, it wasn't as punishing as my husband's anal abuse in the past. And because of that, I let The Explorer explore.

The way The Explorer had my thigh cocked, it left my pussy wide open for Assad, who buried his manhood deep inside of me, just as The Explorer began to pull back out of my anus. These two gentlemen kept crowding me in this mesmerizing rhythm—one went in as the other pulled out.

They were seesawing my orifices.

"Oh yes!" I cried out. "Fill me up! Both of yall keep it in me please! Ouuuw, yes!"

My hysteria spurred them on. They dug deeper, faster, more aggressive. I was dripping in sweat, as were they. One

of them peeled my blindfold off, but the pleasure was too intense for me to open my eyes just yet.

"Look at me," Assad whispered.

I opened my eyes, but they were still narrow and dreamy. In front of me, Assad touched his forehead to mine—but his eyes were still closed. I wondered why he asked me to look at him ... when suddenly the voice came again.

From behind: "Look at me," Assad whispered again.

Startled, I jerked my head over my shoulder and was shocked to see another Assad Blackwell glaring at me passionately, as he grinded in and out of my booty.

"Look at me ..."

I stopped typing right there, proud of what I had written so far. The purpose of this erotic dream sequence of the two Assad Blackwells was to show the reader how infatuated Andrea was with him. She hadn't had sex with Assad in real life yet, but her thoughts were so inundated with his chocolateness that she began to have dreams at night of him and a clone gangbanging her. Sometimes daydreams.

I closed my laptop shut, setting it on the nightstand. Thanks to Rayshawn Meeks and Faheem Mathis, I was able to get through that chapter without any writer's block.

Five minutes later my bedroom door opened. It was Patricia. She must have seen on the camera monitor that I was finished typing.

"How'd your writing go?" she asked me, as she came and sat down on the edge of my bed.

"Fantastic."

"So Faheem and Rayshawn really helped, huh?"

"Yep. More than I thought. My writing always moves along at a faster pace when I've actually experienced what I'm writing about."

"So how are you feeling?"

I paused at that question, knowing exactly what she was asking. The threesome with Faheem and Rayshawn was my first since the traumatic one I'd experienced with Isaiah and Delana.

"I feel fine," I told her.

"You sure?" She touched my leg.

"Yes. Isaiah and that ho Delana popped in my head once, but I was having too much fun with the film brothas to let those thoughts ruin a good time."

She arched an eyebrow. "You know we still have to go through with this, right? You're not too attached, are you?"

"To Rayshawn? No."

"Faheem too," she said.

"Not Faheem," I said vehemently. "We're not touching him. He doesn't believe I'm a killer."

"But you do agree that Rayshawn has to go, right? He broke into our home—twice!"

I sighed. "Rashawn ... Yes, he has to go."

163

"He knows about the ring. He saw the ring. You can't back out of this, Phaedra. He—"

"I said yes!"

Patricia blinked. She seemed to be second-guessing my resolve.

"I just want happiness," I said to her, whining. "I deserve happiness after all I've been through. I don't wanna hurt anybody else after this."

"I need you to really consider Faheem also ... I like him too, Phaedra, and I know he's the closest you've gotten to a real Assad, but when Rayshawn comes up missing he's gonna look at us."

"No he won't."

"How can you be so sure?"

I reached for my laptop, pulling it back onto the bed. I was going to show her another fool-proof crime I typed up—one that would make Isaiah and Delana's tragedies look like child's play.

Chapter 23: Rayshawn Meeks

My foot was no longer in a brace. I had just come from the doctor with instructions to refrain from any enduring physical activity on my feet (as if that was a problem). Next week I had another x-ray scheduled to make sure the ligaments and tendons around the bone were healing okay.

"Call Faheem Mathis," I pronounced carefully, because my phone always had trouble with his name.

This time though my phone locked onto the contact without a hitch, so I placed my phone on the center console and tapped speakerphone. Usually I would have my phone synced to whatever car I was driving, but this was my first time in a Tesla Model S and its 17-inch infotainment system was a little intimidating. You would think a vehicle as tech-based as this would automatically sync it for me.

My phone rang twice.

"Hello?" Faheem answered.

"How'd the meeting go?" I asked.

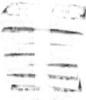

"Phaedra Hodges is rocking with us," he declared, full of enthusiasm. "It's official. She signed the contract right there in front of me, and a representative from her publishing company signed as well. We just walked out of the conference room and I'm getting in my car now. I'm tryna hurry up and leave so she won't change her mind."

I laughed. "Too bad I couldn't be there."

"You had the doctor's appointment, right? Did he straighten you out?"

"No more foot brace. I'm in the Tesla now, looking down at my bare left foot because it's still a little uncomfortable in shoes and socks."

"TMI," he said.

"Hey, fuck you. My feet are pretty."

"Not the ones I saw in Phaedra's room last month," he joked.

"Oh, that reminds me ..." I paused, trying to figure out how to word it. "You know that whole time we was in her room ..."

"What about it?"

"It's not all that important but ... I just wanted to let you know I wasn't giving Phaedra my all." I was trying to explain the discrepancy in the lengths of our johnsons. "I wasn't as erect as I normally am."

"Shawty, why the fuck are you telling me this?! I don't give a fuck what you was doing. I was worried about gettin' mines off."

"I know. I was too."

"Was you lookin' at my meat or somethin'?"

"Nah," I lied.

"Phaedra asked about you in the meeting."

"She did?!" There was no hiding my excitement.

"Yep. She wanted to know why you wasn't there. I told her about yo doctor's appointment and that you'd probably be at home resting after that."

"Is she trying to get down and dirty again?"

I hadn't had sex with Phaedra since the threesome. Faheem hadn't either, he said. I talked to her on the phone since then, a couple three-way conference calls with her and Faheem, but the conversation was all business. No freaky stuff. It was as if the orgy never happened. And I didn't like that. I wanted another taste.

I had also dropped my quest to prove that she and Patricia were murderers. The more I thought about it, the more ridiculous it seemed. Who would jeopardize their freedom by dropping clues to their crime in a bestselling book? Nobody, especially not Phaedra Hodges. She wasn't a killer. She was just a damn good novelist.

"Phaedra hasn't brought up sex and I haven't either," Faheem informed me. "And you better not be pressing her either. I'm sure if she needs our services again, she'll let us know. How's Natasha?"

He threw in my girlfriend's name to make me feel guilty.

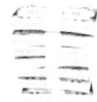

"She's cool," I said, disappointed. "She's at home, probably watching *Little Women: Atlanta.*"

"Tell her I said hi. And don't forget to plug in the Tesla overnight. We need it at the studio fully charged first thing in the morning."

"Will do, boss."

"A'ight, you take it easy," he said. Then: "Oh wait. I wanted to tell you somethin' ..."

"What?"

"Words of encouragement: It's not the size of the boat that counts; it's the motion in the ocean, you ol' little dick ass nigga."

"Hey, fuck—!"

But his derisive laughter cut me off and he hung up in my face.

***

I parked the Tesla in my garage, then climbed out of the driver's seat. I remembered to plug the charging adapter into the rear taillight of the car, then I walked around the rear end and up to the door that led into the house. I unconsciously put more weight on my right foot, even though the doctor told me to start trusting my left more.

"Natasha," I called out, as I set my keys on the storage bench in the hallway.

She didn't answer me. But I heard the TV on upstairs. Then, deciding to listen to my doctor's advice, I walked to the stairs while leading with my left foot. The pain was minor.

Trust the process, Rayshawn, I heard the doctor telling me. Then—*slip!*

My left foot suddenly thrust high into the air as if I kicked an invisible ball and missed, and I landed hard on my back.

"Ahhh shit," I groaned. The wind had been knocked out of me. "Natasha! Help!"

I laid there on the hardwood floor for a moment, then pushed myself up to a sitting position. It was then that I noticed the red stain I had slipped on; it was now a streak.

And it looked like blood.

"Natasha!" I called again, louder.

I wasn't concerned—yet. But as I got to my feet and started upstairs, I noticed a growing trail of blood on every step. My first thought was, *Her period snuck up on her.* Then, once I reached the second floor, I saw a sickening amount of blood soaked into the carpet, all over the floor, leading into the master bedroom.

"Natasha!" I screamed, as I ran into our room, no longer feeling the pain in my foot.

I paused at the door. I was staring at Natasha's bloody body crumpled on the ground next to the bed.

I hurried over, dropping to my knees beside her. "What happened, baby?" I asked, my voice trembling as I unfolded her body in my arms so I could see her bloody face.

Her eyes were open. But she was staring at the ceiling blankly. She was dead.

"Natasha, no!" I screamed, as I cradled her in my arms, crying.

I couldn't believe this. She couldn't be dead. I hadn't had a chance to be good to her!

I heard a noise behind me.

Jerking my head around, I saw my bedroom door slowly swinging closed, revealing the person that was hiding behind it.

It was Patricia West.

I was struck with horror. Patricia was covered in blood—in Natasha's blood!

"Rayshawn Meeks, 35-year-old film producer and known philanderer," Patricia began in an eerie tone, "pummels his longtime girlfriend to death for accusing him of cheating."

I looked at the side of her leg. She was hiding something behind her leg. A weapon, I was sure.

"Patricia, why did you do this to her?!" I hollered.

Patricia ignored me. From behind her big leg, she revealed an all-black pump-action shotgun. She raised it, gripping it in both hands. The barrel was pointed at me.

"Reports have come in from several different women claiming that they've had sexual relationships with the producer," Patricia went on in that same weird cadence, as if she were reading from a script. "They all claim he was aggressive, but none thought he was capable of murdering his own girlfriend."

"Patricia, you don't have to do this," I pleaded. "I'm sorry for breaking into you and Phaedra's home. I don't care what yall did no more. It was none of my business. Her husband deserved it. His side chick probably did too. But I don't deserve this, Patricia. Natasha didn't deserve this!"

She cocked the shotgun. *Click-clack.*

"Rayshawn Meeks is still missing," she continued. "If you have any idea of his whereabouts, please call the—"

I lunged at Patricia to grab the shotgun, a desperate attempt to save my own life.

Boom!

171

Chapter 24: Rayshawn Meeks

I felt the pain in my chest before I could open my eyes. It was a struggle just to get my eye lids at half-mast. Vision blurred, I stared at a concrete floor with one side of my face pasted to it. It was cold. And the air smelled dusty and dank ... the smells from an ancient basement.

"Urghh, fuck ..." I groaned.

The only part of my body I had the strength to move was my left arm, because I was partially laying on my right, due to me being placed or thrown or dropped here on my side. I brought my hand up to the chest of my Ralph Lauren button-down, where I thought Patricia had blasted me with shotgun shrapnel. But as I rubbed my chest from shoulder blade to shoulder blade, I felt no gaping wounds, just bruises.

She must have used some other ammunition besides shells, I thought. *A bean bag round, perhaps. It had to be something*

non-deadly with enough stopping power to knock me out cold. But why didn't she kill me?

"Help," I muttered, as I tried to move my feet.

"You're wasting your breath," a male voice responded. "You're in the basement of an eight thousand square foot mansion. If you yelled for help *upstairs*, no one would be able to hear you. Down here, you're shit out of luck—times ten."

I couldn't see him. I couldn't move. "Who are you?" I asked.

"My name is Isaiah Hodges. I'm Phaedra's husband."

I felt the sensations of panic and shock coursing through my body, but none of my muscles moved.

"I've been trapped down here in this cage for two years, going on three," he revealed.

"We're in a cage?" I asked.

"Yep. Separate cages. I'm in my own cage. And you have your own cage. There was enough room over here for them to put you with me, but they wanted us separate, for whatever reason. So they went through the trouble to build another one."

"They built cages? What kinda people ..." I struggled to formulate words because I was still short of breath. "... would do something like this?"

"People like me," Isaiah said with a heavy sigh.

I didn't understand. My head throbbed with pain the more I tried to figure out why I was still alive.

174

"I'm the one who built the cage that I'm in now," Isaiah explained. "I built it for Phaedra. Whenever she pissed me off, I would drag her ass down here into the basement and lock her in this cage for hours. Sometimes I left her down here overnight. I'd get drunk and forget about her. So to answer your question: people like me build cages to put their spouse in when they don't see eye to eye."

I found the strength to roll onto my back. It felt better here, staring up at the metal roof of my cage. It looked about four feet up, so even if I was physically able to stand, I wouldn't be able to rise to my full height.

Then suddenly my pain shifted, and it felt like there was a crushing weight pressing down on my chest. I tried my damnedest to sit up. And I did, after much pain-staking effort. I scooted on my behind until my back rested against the rear bars of my cage, for spine support. My clothes were powdered gray with dust.

"What's your name?" Isaiah asked me.

I looked over at him, finally. Off instinct, I winced at his appearance. I had seen pictures of Isaiah in the paper and on the internet, him standing about 6'5" in a tailored designer suit, looking magnificent and rich. But now he was just skin and bones. His face was sunken. He couldn't have been older than 45, but he looked 60. The hair on his head was matted and nappy. So was his beard.

But one thing I noted was that, if he had been trapped down here for years, all of his hair should have been longer.

Someone had been grooming him.

"What's your name, nigga?" he asked again, more hostile.

"Rayshawn Meeks."

"Rayshawn, huh?" He paused, as if deciding whether or not my name met his qualifications. "Rayshawn ... You fucked my wife."

I didn't know how to respond. My first thought was to lie, like always.

But he pointed one of his scrawny fingers outside his cage. "I watched you fuck Phaedra on that TV right there. Live, in HD."

I looked. There was a flat screen television—30 or 40 something inches—mounted to the old, crumbly gray concrete wall. The screen was black. It was shut off.

"You fucked her a couple months ago by yourself," he added. "And then about a month ago you and a friend of yours fucked her at the same time."

"I ... I'm sorry," I said.

"No you're not. You're not sorry."

I didn't know if I was remorseful for screwing his wife or not. But I was sorry that I was here. Sorry that I was in so much pain.

"I probably watched fifty men fuck Phaedra since I've been down here," Isaiah said. "But the way you and your friend fucked her ... I think that hurt the worst."

"She makes you watch who she has sex with?" I asked in disbelief.

"I don't have to watch. I can close my eyes. I used to close my eyes or put my head down whenever that TV popped on and I saw another man being invited into my wife's bed. But now I feel compelled to watch. It's part of my punishment. Sometimes I cry as I watch. That's how petty Phaedra is. This is payback for all the women I cheated on her with. For all the evil shit I've ever done to her."

I watched him pick up a magazine from the piles strewn about in his cage. He showed me the cover to the one he held—it was an *Essence* magazine with Phaedra Hodges on the front, smiling, holding her paperback book *Petty*.

"She throws every magazine she's ever been featured in, into my cage," he said. "She wants me to see how successful she is without me in her life. I told her that I was proud of her a thousand times. She still won't let me go. I think she wants me to die in here. She hasn't killed me yet because she still loves me."

"Why am I here?" I asked him desperately.

He chuckled. "Obviously you did something to Phaedra that you wasn't supposed to. So you tell me why you're here."

And then both of our heads suddenly turned when the basement door opened at the top of the stairs.

Up Next from Keesh:

Rich & Petty 2

The following is an excerpt from Go Jordan's:

Married to a Demon

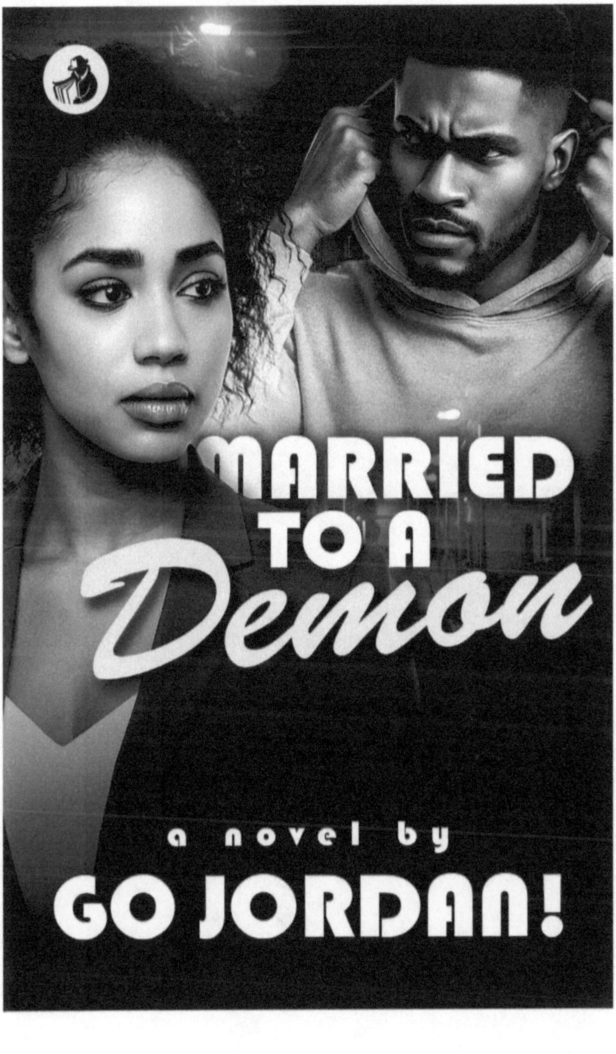

Chapter 1

I eased my Jaguar F-Pace down the long gravel road, the LED beams of my headlights piercing through the darkness. Pebbles crunched beneath my new Pirelli tires.

"If I ever catch a flat on these sharp ass rocks, I'm suing yo ass," I said, as if he could hear me. "For every kilo you got."

Up ahead, Sidney Frazier's old antebellum-style house came into view, barely lit within the darkness. I squinted, because I thought I saw somebody sitting on the white porch. And as I got closer, I realized my 38-year-old eyes weren't deceiving me yet. There was a shape hunched in the rocking chair, unmoving.

I parked, but let my engine idle. "Wussup, you grumpy old bastard?" I said out the window. "You betta not be sleep either. Out here slippin'. You probably just got through jacking off. Lonely ass nigga."

No response. The silence was eerie, especially with my engine only emitting a low, refined purr.

I shut the car off and climbed out, my Chuck Taylors crushing gravel as I approached Sidney's home. Then a weird feeling came over me. Something wasn't right. Sidney sat slumped in the rocking chair, his head lolled back at an

unnatural angle. His gray-streaked cornrows were messier than normal, strands sticking out, with his wrinkled face seeming even more gaunt and hollow. His thick mustache now hung limp and lifeless above his parted lips.

"Sid? C'mon, wake up. I can't stay long, bro. I got moves to make, big homie."

I reached out, gripping Sidney's shoulder. Cold. Stiff.

Recoiling, I realized that my mentor was actually dead. I didn't see any signs of foul play either. He must've passed in his sleep.

"Damn, Sid ... it was that time, huh?"

My gaze fell to the old man's lap, and there it was—the kilo of cocaine, wrapped in plastic. I plucked it from underneath my longtime friend's dead hands. I sure wasn't leaving it. This was my livelihood, for now.

I looked at Sidney again, shaking my head. "Shoulda listened to me 'bout those cigarettes, old man. I told you they was gon' kill you."

No matter how much I had nagged Sidney about cigarettes—even before we both got out of prison—he'd just give me that stubborn look and keep puffing away. One day on the yard, Sidney started hacking up a lung, bent over and wheezing, struggling to catch his breath. I clapped him on his back, telling him to quit or he'd die in prison.

Sidney had finally caught his breath, and as soon as he did, he took another long drag from his cigarette, the ember

184

flaring bright orange. Smoke poured from his nostrils as he rasped, "You think these cigarettes will kill me? Jordan, I've been trying to die for years. But while I'm here, I'ma do what I wanna do. You can count on that shit."

Now, as I stared at his dead body, I let out a sad chuckle.

"Gonna miss you, Sid. You were the realest ... Thanks for everything. Fa-real, big homie."

Clutching the package of cocaine, I glanced around, making sure no one was watching me. Not that there ever was anybody out here in the middle of Tonganoxie, Kansas. I turned and headed for my car, the kilo tucked under my arm.

As I opened the trunk and threw the kilo inside, my mind started racing. Where was I gonna get more dope after this brick ran out?

But then again, did I really need any more drugs?

I stood there for a moment, staring at Sidney's lifeless body. "You kept your word, though. You helped me pay for my divorce lawyer, just like you promised. But damn, I was hoping you'd keep supplying me until the divorce was final." I shook my head, realizing something. "Maybe this is your way of forcing me to quit hustling, old man. You always said you didn't want me back in the game for long. Guess you're making sure I stick to it, even from the other side."

Reaching under the trunk floor, I retrieved a crinkled brown paper bag stuffed with hundred dollar bills and took

it over to Sidney's chair. I tucked the bag inside of his faded flannel shirt, pushing it down deep so it wouldn't fall out.

"There you go, big homie," I said, patting his chest. "You know I always pay my debts. Thanks for looking out."

I returned to the trunk and slammed it shut, taking one last look at Sidney's motionless body slumped in the rocking chair before turning away. Sliding behind the wheel of my Jag, I push-started the engine and threw it in reverse. Gravel crunched again as I backed out of the long driveway, the headlights sweeping across Sidney's porch in an eerie farewell.

Chapter 2

"Thank you for showing up today," the teacher opened in a boisterous tone. His friendly face crinkled around the eyes as he smiled. "My name's Samuel Harris. You all can call me Sam. I know being here for a mandatory parenting class isn't exactly how you all wanted to spend your Saturday, but I promise to make it as fun and engaging as possible."

He began pacing around the classroom, making eye contact with each of us. "To kick things off, I'm going to assign everyone a number from one to seven. When I point at you, just say the next available number out loud."

The teacher pointed at a young woman in the front row. "You're number one."

He continued moving through the classroom, assigning each person a number in sequential order. When his finger landed on me, he said, "Seven."

Once everyone had a number, the teacher clapped his hands together. "Excellent! Now, I want you all to find the others who have the same number as you and form groups of three. Those will be your teams for various activities throughout the day."

Chairs squeaked against the linoleum floor as people began shuffling around, trying to locate their group members. I scanned the room, searching for the other two sevens.

"Over here!" A pretty, athletic-looking woman with rich mahogany skin waved me over.

I made my way towards her. "Seven?" I asked.

"That's me," she said with a warm smile. "I'm Makeda."

"I'm Jordan." I shook her hand. "Nice to meet you, Makeda. Under these circumstances."

"Likewise. Because I can think of better ways to spend a Saturday than being reminded of my failed marriage."

"Yeah, me too."

As I took a seat beside her, another woman joined our small circle—a blonde with a rounded face and a gentle presence. "Hi, I'm Audrey. Looks like we're all lucky number sevens."

"Lucky?" Makeda scoffed. "I'll count myself lucky if I don't have to pay this broke-ass negro I married alimony."

Sam's voice boomed over the murmurs of conversation. "Alright, everyone settled in their groups? Fantastic! Let's start with some icebreakers. Let's go around and introduce ourselves. Tell us your name, what you do for a living, and maybe an interesting fact about yourself." He pointed to Makeda. "Why don't you start us off?"

"My name is Makeda Woodard. I work as a senior correctional officer at Leavenworth Federal Penitentiary. An interesting fact ..." Makeda sat up straighter. "Well, I'm highly skilled in self-defense techniques. A video of me breaking up a fight between inmates actually went viral a few years back."

Sam raised his eyebrows. "Now that's one of the most interesting things I've heard since I started teaching this class. And I've been doing it for twenty-three years."

Makeda flashed a self-assured smile. "I got a little fame, but I didn't let it go to my head. After that video, my *husband* all of a sudden wanted to do videos together and steal my clout—"

Sam cut her off, gesturing to Audrey next. "And you are?"

"Audrey Baxter," she said softly. "I'm a stay-at-home mom." A faint blush colored her cheeks as all eyes turned to her.

"The most important job of all," the teacher stated. "Any interesting facts?"

Her voice wavered slightly as she said, "An interesting fact about me is that I have my own Cricut machine, and I make custom shirts and hats to sell online. It's ... it's my only source of income right now." Her eyes shone with the start of tears.

Sam's expression softened with sympathy. "Running a small business from home while caring for your family is an incredible feat, Audrey. You should be proud of using your creativity and skills to support your household." He gave her an encouraging nod before turning to me. "And you are?"

"Jordan Bell. I'm an author."

His eyes lit up with interest. "An author? What kind of books do you write?"

I hesitated, not wanting to scare these folks with talks of crime and street politics. "Urban fiction," I said. "Stories that talk about the underbelly of society."

"Ooh, like stuff for mature readers?" The teacher nodded sagely. "Sounds fascinating. And that's what you do for a living? It's your main source of income?"

"Yes," I said. "I plan to write forever and ever, if I can. I enjoy the whole process."

"Wow. Your occupation alone is an interesting fact. But you're more than welcome to share another one."

"Another one? Uh ..."

I had a lot of interesting facts. I went to jail when I was 19 for armed robbery, didn't get out until I turned 27. I married my wife the first day I got out of jail, because she stood by me toward the end of my sentence. Looking back, I wished I would've blocked her from my visiting list, but hey—I was trying to turn a new leaf. Once I decided to divorce her, I started selling dope to prepare for war. Because Sidney told me divorce was war, and untraceable cash was king. After I sold my first kilo, I retained a lawyer and filed for divorce. I had planned to have more money stashed before I filed, but I jumped the gun—I couldn't stand that bitch no more.

I addressed the class: "Interesting fact … let's see … Uh, I haven't been on social media in over a year because it distracts me from my writing."

"Well, I guess that means you won't be tweeting about our class discussions anytime soon," Sam said with a playful grin, earning a few chuckles from the class. As the laughter subsided, he held up a hand. "But in all seriousness, let me be very clear about something. The topics we'll cover in this parenting class can be extremely sensitive and personal. Nothing we discuss here leaves this room."

A hush fell over the room as the weight of his words sank in. Sam paused, letting the warning linger for a moment.

"If I discover that someone has posted something online about what gets said here, there will be serious consequences. You could face removal from the class, fines, or even legal action depending on the severity."

Sam continued calling on other members of the class to share their introductions. As the attention shifted away from our group, Makeda turned to me with an intrigued expression.

"So, Jordan, you write urban fiction, huh? You ever think about doing a book on Kamau and Neeta Bryant?"

"Who?" I asked.

"You mean to tell me that you write about crime and never heard of Kamau and Neeta Bryant? They're like the modern day Bonnie and Clyde with a drug empire that spans

from California to Honduras. Bless your heart, Jordan. I can't believe you never heard of them. But I guess I'll give you the benefit of the doubt. You did say you haven't been on the internet in a while."

I used the internet every day, just not social media. My temporary return to a criminal lifestyle made staying off those platforms necessary. I didn't correct her, though. I wanted to hear more.

"Well, I have a confession," she went on. "I didn't hear about neither one of 'em until they brought Kamau to Leavenworth. I'm one of the few guards there that's cleared to even be around Kamau. I noticed that the other inmates worship him like he's some sort of a god. But if you look on the internet, all the news people and bloggers say he's a demon."

"And they let you around him?" I asked.

"Let me? I'm a senior muthafuckin' correctional officer. I go where I please in that bitch. I talk to Kamau every day at work. I'm practically the only one that can transport him through the facility. From what I've seen, he's cool, down to earth, funny, intelligent—*real* intelligent. There's something about him that draws people in. He doesn't seem like a killer at all. That's not saying much, though. You'll be surprised by the people I've come across that don't look like killers, but are."

"Why do they have him in a federal prison? What did he get convicted of?"

"That's the thing—he hasn't been convicted yet. Normally, he'd be held at Wyandotte County Jail until he goes to trial. But Kamau is considered an extremely high-risk nigga. Wyandotte County's facilities just aren't up to par."

"They think he's gonna escape?" I asked.

"Yep. Leavenworth has much tighter security. Reinforced concrete cells, higher staff-to-inmate ratios, state-of-the-art surveillance, shit like that. Their screening procedures are tighter too. We're built to contain the most dangerous offenders until their cases go to trial. So even though he's technically just awaiting trial, the U.S. Marshals felt it was safest to have Kamau housed at a federal facility."

From there, Makeda told me how Kamau's wife, Neeta Bryant, was born into the notorious Crenshaw Mafia gang back in LA. Her brother Murk was high up in the ranks, selling kilos all over the city.

I hung on her every word. *Kilos?* I thought. *That's just what I need right about now.* But I pushed that thought aside.

Makeda said that Neeta crossed paths with Kamau at Georgia State University while they were both in college, and Neeta supposedly lured him into her brother's drug trafficking business. They eventually built their own empire by overthrowing a Honduran drug plantation.

My interest was piqued. "Is Neeta locked up too?" I asked.

Audrey, the plump blonde, unexpectedly chimed in. "I heard Neeta got shot point-blank in Honduras. They say she's dead, but they never found her body. I read about it on a fan page dedicated to them."

"See, look at that. Even the white girl heard of 'em." Makeda gave Audrey's arm a gentle squeeze. "Jordan, their story is begging to be told. You better listen to me. And if you write that book and it takes off, I want a cut for telling you about it."

The teacher clapped his hands, drawing our attention back to the front of the room. "Okay, now that we've all gotten to know each other a little better, it's time for our first discussion on the impact that divorce has on our children ..."

As the teacher droned on about positive co-parenting strategies and the effects of exposing children to conflict, all I could focus on was the story of Kamau and Neeta. Since Makeda held a high-ranking position at Leavenworth, maybe she could arrange a meeting with Kamau himself by adding me to his visitor list. Meeting Kamau could potentially open new avenues for me. I'd been wanting to write a true crime book for a while now. Something different than the fiction I normally wrote.

After the parenting class ended, we all had to wait in line to receive our certificates, which was a legal requirement before a judge could grant a divorce decree in Missouri. I took the opportunity to ask Makeda if she knew exactly what Kamau was being charged with.

Makeda's face scrunched up as she thought about it. "You know, I'm not a hundred percent sure on all the charges. I know there's conspiracy to traffic drugs across state lines, and money laundering too. But my superiors were really tight-lipped about the details when he first arrived. They just told all of us that he was dangerous."

"He has at least one murder charge coming down the line," Audrey chimed in again. "Kamau and his wife killed a woman that used to work for them."

"Oh yeah, Vida Benitez," said Makeda. "I heard about that too. Vida was cold as ice. She was down for the Crenshaw Mafia, until she saw an opportunity to take over, and she grabbed it. Vida ended up selling the Bryants out to save her own ass."

"So would you two be interested in telling me more about their story over drinks?" I asked. "Maybe we could go out to a bar after this and yall can fill me in on what you know? I'm buying. Call it an early celebration of our new-found single life."

Makeda said, "You had me at 'I'm buying.' I could use a strong drink after this parenting class shitshow."

"Oh gosh, I'd love to join you two, but I don't have a way to get there," Audrey said in an apologetic tone. "My sister is keeping my kids overnight, so I'm free. But I had to catch an Uber here from Independence, and I have to catch one home. They charge extra for multiple stops and I don't have that kind of money right now. The judge ordered my ex to pay my legal fees, but he—"

I cut her off. "I'll take you home. Independence? That ain't a problem."

I could see the hesitation in Audrey's eyes. "Are you sure? You're already buying drinks. I really don't want to be a bother."

"I insist. The only bother would be if you didn't come along. And your company more than makes up for a little extra time behind the wheel."

Makeda chuckled beside us. "He's not gonna take no for an answer, Audrey. Put the kids out of your mind and be selfish for a change."

Audrey's lips curved into a shy smile. "I guess I'm out-numbered here. Thank you, Jordan. I really appreciate you going out of your way."

"Think nothing of it," I replied.

We decided on a little hole-in-the-wall bar on Westport that Makeda said had the best whiskey. After we got our signed certificates and headed outside, I told Makeda we'd follow her. She slid into a sleek, black Dodge Charger with tinted windows and chrome rims. The car suited her—it was powerful and commanded attention. As me and Audrey pulled out of the parking lot behind her in my Jaguar SUV, I couldn't help but feel a thrill of anticipation. Not only was I going to learn more about a demon named Kamau Bryant, but I was also going to spend more time with the woman whose prison clearance could potentially transform my writing career.

Thank you for reading!

Please leave a review. It truly helps. And if you really-really enjoyed it, write "Go Jordan!" at the end of your review. Much love!

Then visit:

www.felonybooks.com

And stay updated on all of Felony Books' *newest releases, free giveaways,* and *special promotions!*

GRAB THIS ONE!

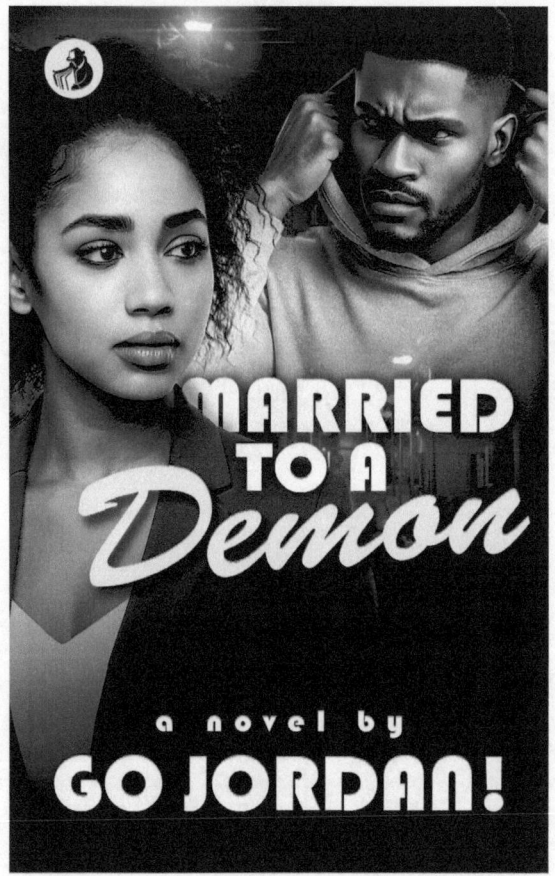

Married to a Demon by Go Jordan!

To fund his divorce, writer Jordan Bell starts selling cocaine again. But when he lands a gig interviewing alleged kingpin Kamau Bryant in federal prison, he uncovers **a love story darker than any fiction he's ever written.**

www.felonybooks.com

ALSO AVAILABLE!

Two Girls One Thug by Jordan Belcher

After hearing his fiancée drown over an illegal prison phone, Irving Mercee is released a year later to start fresh. But beneath the surface, he's dealing drugs and hunting her killer. As he tortures suspects and spirals deeper into violence, two women try to save him through love, unaware **they might become his next victims.**

www.felonybooks.com

www.ingramcontent.com/pod-product-compliance
Lightning Source LLC
Chambersburg PA
CBHW020433180626
46812CB00003B/1203

* 9 7 8 1 9 4 0 5 6 0 3 7 3 *